A DON'T JUDGE A BOOK

NOVEL

D1823023

TICKED

BY

KAREN RAINES

To Tia,
Ride that Rooster!
Karen Raines
—x—

Copyright

Table Of Contents

Copyright   3
Prologue   7
1 – Hanging...   14
2 – There's a new boss in town   20
3 - Don't tic me off   27
4 – She said what now?   33
5 – I have a word for you...   37
6 – Polish cussing is my thang   44
7 – Get into the groove   50
8 – I put a spell on you   55
9 – Road to hell   62
10– No speak English   68
11 – Cat and Mouse   74
12 - Memes explain everything   80
13 – A man with two names   87
14 – Leave a message...   92
15 – Stripper initiation   99
16 – Plucking Feathers   105
17 – Ding, ding, we have a winner   110
18 – There's a cock in my hen house   114
19 – Meet the f***ers   121
20 - One doesn't care   129
21 – I don't wanna talk   137
22 – Damage control   144
23 – The tic that won't quit   150
24 – Making Memories   156
25 – Can't take me anywhere   161
26 – Breaking the rules   166
27 – Blame it on the boogie   172
28 – It isn't what it looks like   178
29 – She started it   188
30 – The fight of my life   196
31 – Well, that told me!   203

32 – At least she's on my side   209
33 – We are family   216
34 – What doesn't kill us...   226
Epilogue   233
Dork To Dirty   239
Acknowledgements   240
About the Author   243
Reading List   243

Prologue

Willow

"I don't like it!"

I smirked over my shoulder at the brooding hulk of man that was currently pacing the floor of the room.

"This was your idea," I reminded him.

He gave me a withering look and continued to wear a hole in the tiles.

"Yeah well, you should know better than to listen to anything I have to say," he rolled his eyes and stopped his frantic pacing, the thumb and finger of his right hand reaching up to pinch the bridge of his nose. "I'm calling it off."

I spun around so fast I nearly lost my footing. "No!"

"No?"

My fists clenched at my sides and his eyes darted down to them. His features softened a touch as he took in my stance.

"Willow," he sighed dramatically and perched on the side of the dressing table behind him.

"Look Daniel, it's not like I'm about to make a career change here."

My cousin-in-law's eyes lit up and his usual wit began to shine through finally. "And what, pray tell, is wrong with this particular career path?"

I raised an eyebrow and gestured to the rows of bright clothing adorning the room. "Well for one thing, this is a male strip club and I just don't have the right junk in my pants."

He laughed heartily and pointed to a huge row labelled *'From Dork To Dirty – keep your fucking hands off!'*.

"Oh, I don't know. I think you'd rock the lab coat and thong."

His laughter was infectious, and I couldn't help but join in as the image of me wearing his costume flitted across my brain.

Turning back to face the wall of mirrors, I took a good long look at what I was wearing and felt a small smile grace my lips. I was a full-on showgirl, complete with feathers in places that didn't like to be tickled in public, if you know what I mean. But it was hot. Seriously hot.

For once my hair was perfectly styled, thanks to Jezebel, the resident stylist.

A guy called Jezebel. That Queen was more like the goddess of hair.

I wasn't a fan of the thick makeup, but he assured me I would be thankful for it under the harsh spotlights I was about to be showered with on the stage.

The thought of those spotlights and the huge crowd they would be sure to hide from my view, at least for a little while, was enough to bring me crashing back down to earth. Shit, maybe he was right. Maybe I shouldn't do this.

"I'm just worried. What sort of a friend would I be if I wasn't. I know this is a one-time deal, I know it was all my idea. But I'm starting to feel a little sick thinking about you getting your kit off out there for the masses."

"You mean it's just dawned on you that if my cousin found out about this you'd be a eunuch?"

"I love my balls!"

"I know, you get them out every time you're drunk and sing to them."

8

"They deserve the love," he declared solemnly and gave his groin a little pat to prove his point.

Not that I was going to admit this to him, especially while he was freaking out about his boys, but I was a bit worried about his wife Simone finding out too. She wasn't just my big cousin, she was my best friend, my confidant and my biggest supporter.

She was also my biggest protector.

This little stunt of mine was right up there with the time I ran off to some club in a shady part of London and lied to her about it. She had found me in the early hours of the morning, having threatened everyone I knew within an inch of their lives and dragged me out of that club.

She got me grounded for a month.

I was 19 years old at the time.

Lame... and extremely sheltered.

Now while I loved her for caring, and let's face it, she cared a million times more than my parents, all the mollycoddling had done was stop me from finding my own way in life.

Dramatic? Cut me some slack, I'm about to get my lala's out for a room full of horny men.

"I think I'm gonna be sick."

Daniel was a blur of motion as he grabbed a bin and held it out to me. It was kinda sweet, so I took it from him and dropped it to the floor.

"Metaphorically," I clarified and there went his eyes again.

His thumb and finger went back to rubbing the space between his eyes and I went back to my inner battle between right and wrong.

"I'm calling up to Mr. E," he said quietly, referring to the club owner. "This was a stupid idea. You aren't ready to do something like this, I don't know what I was thinking suggesting it in the first place."

"Dan…" I began but he held a hand up and carried on talking above me.

"What if you freak out? What if you trip and fall? What if someone manages to lay a hand on you? What if you start to…"

"Stop!" I shouted.

He paused and waited, his speech halted because if there was one thing I could guarantee about the cocky, sarcastic and often egotistical man in front of me, it was that he always listened to what I had to say. He was the only one that did.

I kinda loved the bastard for that. Don't tell anyone.

"I know you worry. I know I'm different from other girls," I swallowed thickly, determined not to let my emotions get the best of me. "But wasn't that exactly why we came up with this plan? To push me out of my comfort zone? To help me boost my confidence?"

"Like you need any help with your confidence. You're a loud mouth."

I gave a little curtsey and those damn feathers tickled against the inside of my thighs. Seriously, who comes up with these costumes?

"That stage out there is my worst nightmare. You know that. All those people staring at me, watching my every move… I have to see if I can do it. If for no other reason than that, you need to let me do this."

Our eyes locked, his fiercely protective gaze didn't waver even as we heard the soft click of the door opening and the pulsing beat of the music drift into the room. It closed quickly, and I knew without looking who it was that had joined us.

"What's it gonna be, cuz?" I whispered desperately.

His jaw worked as he pondered, his need to help me warring with the need to protect. I could see the scales tipping against me and I made a split-second decision.

"Ok, I get it. I'm really not trying to get your bollocks chopped off," I chuckled and gave him a pat on his arm. "So why don't we let fate decide."

His head cocked to the side. "And how exactly would we do that?"

Smiling broadly, I turned my head and gave a nod in the direction of our guest. "We'll let him decide."

Daniel smirked as if he knew this was going to be a done deal and my stomach dropped. Oh shit, what if I had this all figured out wrong?

"I think that's the best thing I've heard all night!" He clapped his hands together and rubbed them cheekily, looking every inch the devil. "What do you say, brother? Are we gonna let our girl go out there?"

My eyes closed briefly as I collected my courage. This was it. My whole evening, this whole experiment of mine was on the verge of being shelved. All the weeks of training and learning the routine, the mental preparation, all of it were on the line. It was down to him now.

Benjamin Hope.

He stood with his back to the door, his body leaning against it and his arms crossed over his chest. One boot clad foot was casually crossed over the other as he silently watched the showdown between myself and his brother.

Benjamin Hope, the one man who knew better than anyone what it was like to live with something that stopped you from going for what you wanted. In his case, it had been crippling shyness. My case however was very, very different.

His deep chocolate eyes searched my own, for what I wasn't sure. His fingers rubbed across his stubbled jaw, a contemplative look on his handsome features.

"I think this was a ridiculous idea."

Defeated, my shoulders dropped and I reached for the feather headdress that was sat upon my curly locks.

"However, since you're already in costume it would be rude to back out."

"What?" Daniel shouted at the same time an excited squeal ripped from my throat.

I bounced in place and my fist shot into the air, pumping up and down in celebration.

"Fuck yeah!" I sang loudly.

"See?" Daniel implored, turning to his brother in horror. "This is a bad fucking idea Ben."

I frowned and brought my hand down to rest on my hip, cocking it out to the side and adopting my starting pose for the routine I had memorised. My defiant gaze slammed into the pair of them and I saw the moment Daniel gave in. He groaned and leaned next to his brother, muttering about his poor balls. Ben smiled broadly and shook his head.

"Thank you, Ben."

He winked and opened the door. "Welcome to

Hot Steppers Willow."

1 – Hanging...

Perry

With a groan, I reached over to the bedside table and hit the snooze button. The glaring digits screamed silently at me to get up. My head however, had other ideas.

"I'm never fucking drinking again," I groaned sulkily.

I blamed this all on my gracious host Annie. The woman was a force to be reckoned with. I swear the only reason she and her long-suffering husband Jason made such a great team was because he is the most laid-back person on the planet. He needed to be.

I had finally gotten back to town two days ago and already she had done her bit to lead me astray. Welcome to Reading – the pissed edition.

No matter how much my head was protesting my like for the woman, I couldn't bring myself to hate her. If it wasn't for her, I would be back at my parents right now, and that would have been a fate worse than the hangover from hell.

Heavy footsteps pounded the floor outside my room, followed swiftly by a thud on the bedroom door.

"Get up bitch, it's a school day."

"Fuck off," I yelled back, immediately wishing I hadn't when my temple throbbed.

A deep chuckle sounded through the door. "Yeah, I hear ya. My wife is the devil."

With a roll of my eyes, I forced my legs to leave the bed. If I was gonna face this day, I needed coffee. Lots of coffee.

✓✓✓

I looked good considering how hungover I was. I got ready for my day, feeling sick to my stomach and ashamed to have been out drunk by a woman. A small woman at that. Right now though, the thought of caffeine was the only thing that mattered.

Fucking JD shots.

I walked into the kitchen and was met by a round of wolf whistles from the comedians I was currently rooming with.

"Well look at you all dolled up," Annie cooed as she fed their baby boy in his highchair. At least I think she was meant to be feeding him. Jamie had more food in his hair than in his mouth. The little boy gave me a gummy grin and I smiled back, thinking that the kid was going to be trouble if he turned out anything like his mother.

Jason slid a steaming mug in my direction. I gave him a grateful salute and gulped greedily from the mug.

"You look like I feel," Jason smirked.

I gave him a withering look and carried on gulping down the hot liquid. Coffee made everything better.

"Want some breakfast? I have scrambled eggs and bacon on the go?"

"It's the least you can do," I grumbled, trying to give her my grumpiest look but failing miserably as she stood there in an apron and spatula in hand. "When did you become a 50's housewife?"

"Screw you, you want food or not?"

I chuckled and held my hands in peace. "Yes,

please milady."

Annie set about fixing me a plate while Jason took over feeding the squirming kid. They had quite the routine going which had me smiling inside when I thought back to the good old days. Shit, did we used to get into all kinds of trouble, Annie, me and my older brother Archie. How any of us made it to adulthood was beyond me. Watching this semi domesticated version of the woman that convinced me to smoke my first bong was fucking priceless. Of course, that's what happened when you found your perfect partner in crime, things changed, and for the better.

Shit, what the hell did she put in those shots last night? Here I was, waxing poetic and sounding like a pussy. I gave my head a shake to get rid of the sweet thoughts and instead started to throw out some accusations.

"I can't believe you got me pissed the night before I start my new job." I shook my head in disappointment. "Shame on you Annie."

"Hey," she said. "It's not like I forced them down your throat. You're a big boy now, you could have just said no."

"I'm pretty sure he did say no Annie." Jason interjected on my behalf. Silly fool.

"No, he didn't. I would have remembered."

"Would that be before or after you called him a girl and told him to pull his finger out of his vagina and take one for the team?"

"I have no idea what you're talking about," she sniffed indignantly.

Jason laughed, throwing his head back and then winced. "Ouch, don't make me laugh. It hurts."

16

Seems like I wasn't the only one suffering this morning. It gave me a sick sense of satisfaction.

Annie smirked, enjoying her husband's pain. "See, that's what you get for ganging up on me. Remember our vows? You're supposed to back me up no matter what, in sickness and in health."

"You're definitely sick in the head," I grumbled quietly, earning me a slap across the head from the tea towel.

"Yeah, yeah, whatever you say dear," Jason chuckled, trying to look contrite and failing miserably.

I started eating my breakfast again and listened to the back and forth commentary between the two. It never got old, they really were a match made in heaven. Maybe hell. I wouldn't change them for anything though.

"Anyway," Annie said, turning her attention back to me. "Are you ready for your first day on the job?"

I gave my head a nod as I chewed on my bacon. "Yeah, as ready as I'll ever be. Although it would be nice to know a little bit more about what I would be doing."

"Jasmine told you on the phone what you were going to be doing," she said rolling her eyes. "You're going to be the new Head of Marketing now that Nicole is going on maternity leave. Her absence is gonna leave a massive gap."

I nodded along with her as I chewed on the crispy bacon. She had said as much when I went for the interview.

"There's no way Jasmine can handle being

the head of a department again and be the CEO. It used to eat up all her time, poor thing. Plus, she has a husband to think about now."

I thought about what she was saying and couldn't help but agree. I had only met Jasmine's new husband Ben once at Annie's wedding reception. Jason had nothing but remarkable things to say about him and I figured I'd get to know him better soon, since he was the head of IT at the Gold Dime Group.

"At least I won't have to put up with your sorry ass at work. There's something to be said for maternity leave."

Her eyes narrowed as she pointed that wooden spatula in my face. "Don't get too cocky Mr Moore, there's nothing stopping me coming by every day to bring you a packed lunch. I'm sure I could find something to embarrass you."

"I don't doubt it."

Jason laughed but soon stopped when his wife shot him a menacing look.

"Nothing but love for you babe," the pussy said. I managed not to gag.

"Anyway, this has been great, but I better get my ass in gear." I pushed my chair back and shrugged my suit jacket on. "I'll catch you guys later."

"Good luck son," Jason called in a deep copy of some 70's drama. "I hope the kids are nice to you. If anybody tries to steal your lunch money, make sure you tell the teacher."

"Or beat the shit out of them," Annie yelled. I feared for Jamie's state of mind, poor kid.

"Yeah, yeah, yeah," I laughed as I snatched up my keys and walked to the front door. "Bye Mum, bye Dad."

I smiled all the way to my car and was still smiling when I pulled into the huge car park that belonged to the Gold Dime Group. This was a far cry from my last job and I couldn't wait to get stuck in.

2 – There's a new boss in town

Willow

"Is he still staring?"

"No."

"Are you lying to me?"

"Would I?"

I glared at the side of my friend's face. "All the time."

He laughed. Bastard.

"So, is he still staring."

With a put-out sigh, Owen turned his head to scan the room. "Nope."

I blew out a relieved breath and glanced in the direction of the current subject. He WAS staring!

"You're a lying sack of shit."

"Why ask me to look if you're just going to look for yourself?"

See this was the problem when most of your friends were guys. They just didn't get the girl code thing. If my cousin Simone had been here, this would have been so much simpler.

We stepped towards the counter and placed our usual order for coffees, enjoying the banter with the girls that worked here. It was my absolute go to place, this little treasure of a coffee shop. Oh, there was a large, famous coffee vendor not three doors down, but the locals had stayed loyal to "Coffee Nirvana". It helped that their breakfast muffins were the mutts nuts.

"How are you feeling about today?"

I took a sip of my steaming brew and stood to the side as Owen added enough sugar to rot a tooth to his takeout cup.

"I feel ok. It will be weird not seeing Nicole every day, but she said the new boss is great."

I shrugged, not really knowing what to expect but trusting our team leader's judgement. I worked in the marketing department of Gold Dime Group, a leading advertising agency that was taking the world by storm. Now, we covered all kinds of developments, not just the advertising sides of things. I had been here for 18 months and felt so at home within my department, thanks in large part to our wonderful team leader. Nicole Fuller was a go-getting character, full of ideas and praise. She had worked her ass off to keep our department at the top of its game and although she had an exceptionally busy life, she always made the time to make sure all her employees were ok. She was going to be a tough act to follow.

Today was her last day. Baby number three was on the verge of arriving, something we had all joked about happening during our morning meetings, and she couldn't put off starting her maternity leave any longer. The company had hired externally for her replacement, mainly because no one felt they could live up to her standards.

I felt strangely calm about whoever was going to be taking the reins. Our director, Jasmine Hope, was not a person to mess with within the walls of the company. We all knew that whoever she hired would have the skills to lead our section. Mrs Hope was very protective of the marketing department, since it used to be hers. But that was before my time.

"Um, in the interest of keeping cool," Owen

began, not taking his eyes away from the coffee in front of him. "The staring dude is making his way over here."

Annoyance warred with anxiety inside of me, a dangerous combo for someone that lived my life. I could feel my body tightening down, preparing to lock against its own instincts.

"Hey, I figured I'd come over..."

"No thanks."

He seemed taken aback for a second but regained his thoughts quickly. "You don't know what I was going to..."

"Its fine, I don't need to know. We were just going."

He crossed his arms over his chest and raised his eyebrows. "Ok. There's no need to be a bitch about it."

I could see Owen starting to lose his patience and as grateful as I was for the way my friends backed me up, I had to do these things for myself.

"Listen, again, I apologise for grabbing your hand when I walked in the door. I also apologise, yet again for flicking your lips."

"I kinda liked it," he smirked, taking a step closer.

I held my phone up and flashed the screen in his face. I watched as he read the words, laughed, re-read them and then the moment of clarity as he swept his gaze to my face and saw not an ounce of mockery.

"It's no problem, sorry to have bothered you."

And with that, he scurried away.

Just like they all do.

"Run chicken, don't let the cock win." I yelled, feeling exasperated and yet amused all at the same time.

I flashed the screen of my phone at the startled man standing next to me and waltzed to the door, waving bye to the girls behind the counter. The crisp morning air hit me, blowing away the encounter and replacing it with peace.

"You know, the day you flash your phone and the dude doesn't run, he's gonna be a keeper."

I smiled ruefully. Now that was going to be an interesting day.

✓✓✓

The office was a buzz with the sounds of ringing phones and chatter. It wasn't quite clocking on time and everyone had that Friday feeling going on. I was no exception. I had big plans this weekend, huge, life altering plans. A Star Wars marathon was not to be mocked.

I made my way to my desk and fired up the two pc's that sat side by side. We all had two, well the designers in this department did anyway. There was nothing more frustrating than being in the zone on a design and having to switch over to check the boring mundane shit that we had to deal with too. Hence the second screen, lovingly named the 'Shite Screen'.

A huge stomach came into view before the smiling face of Nicole greeted me. "Morning Will, how are you today my love?"

I smiled up at my boss, my hands automatically reaching out to stroke her baby belly. This happened an awful lot recently, but Nicole was a sweetheart about it and let me get my fill.

"Wow boss, you sure you're gonna make it the day? You look ready to pop."

She groaned and placed a hand at the small of her back. "Not gonna lie, I'm feeling a little on edge today. I wouldn't be surprised if this baby comes before the weekend is over."

"Well, it is your due date on Monday," I laughed.

She rolled her eyes. "Yeah, yeah, you sound like my husband. The boys were both nearly two weeks late though so..."

"Ah yes, but you have an impatient little girl in there now."

She beamed and took my spot on her bump. "If she can just last the day, I'm all set. At least let me get the new guy all set up in here."

I sat back in my chair and glanced around the office. People were settling down to their desks and prepping for the day ahead, the mood in the office still light with that nearly the weekend feeling.

"I wanted to ask you," I began, lowering my voice so as not to attract attention. "When Mr Moore takes over, will I still be in the running to be lead designer for the Gold Tech account?"

I breathed through the anxiety that was threatening to take hold and watched Nicole's face as she answered.

"Absolutely. Jasmine is fully on board with your concept and has already briefed Mr Moore on the state of play with the ongoing projects. There is no reason why he would even consider replacing you. Don't worry."

She placed a hand on top of my head, gave me a small pat with a laughing grin on her face and then walked off to greet everyone else. A relieved sigh escaped my lips. Our company was launching its own brand of tablets and smartphones, the tech involved designed and created by our very own talented IT department. The second I heard about the new project, I knew I wanted in on the marketing. It had been months of research and prep, drawings after drawings and slogans coming out of my ears but I finally handed in my submission, along with three of my colleagues. The feeling of accomplishment when I was picked to lead the team was beyond anything I had ever felt before. They liked my ideas, they liked my statements.

I had been beyond proud.

Determined to make the best impression possible on my new boss, I set to work fine tuning the account I was already working on, making tweaks here and there and becoming lost in the project. It wasn't until sometime later that I heard my name being called and managed to drag my head away from the screen in front of me.

"And here is one of the gems of this department. This is the young lady we've been telling you about."

I smiled up at Nicole and stood awkwardly, my legs fallen asleep from being stuck in the same position for so long.

"Perry Moore, I would like you to meet Willow Summers."

Smiling, I turned to meet my new boss and was met with the deepest brown eyes I had ever seen.

"It's a pleasure to meet you Willow," he crooned in a voice dripping with seduction.

I placed my hand in his, still a little stunned and completely off kilter. I opened my mouth, intending to say hi but instead...

"Get on your knees and nibble my giblets."

3 - Don't tic me off

Willow

Mortified.

That didn't even come close to covering it.

I sat on the closed toilet lid, my face still hot and my heart pounding in my ears as I replayed the scene over and over in my mind. I could still see the stunned look on Mr Moore's face as my mouth threw up the word vomit, completely against my will. I hadn't waited to see what he was going to say in reply, I mean really what was there to say?

I just had a big breakfast?

Luckily, I'm gluten free?

Nope, I calmly excused myself and swiftly made haste towards the hallway, hoping to god that I would make it there before anyone else noticed the craziness that was my body as it went into overdrive.

And now here I was, locked in the ladies, shoulder twitching and fingers flexing out into the ultimate jazz hands. I looked crazy, I knew this. But this, sadly, was the norm for me.

I have Tourette's Syndrome.

It started when I was in primary school, although it was hard to tell since all the kids had gimmicks and unpleasant habits. See that kid picking his nose? See the girl twirling her hair around her finger? How about the kid constantly blinking or the one that keeps wrenching and stretching their mouths as wide as they will go?

Tics. Although most children grow out of these habits, some do not. Some have habits that evolve, become more pronounced. Some say things that they have no control over. Some physically tic, hitting, biting, kicking, flexing, the list is endless, either at themselves or others.

Some people like me.

I was labelled as a naughty child in school, right the way through primary and part of the way through secondary. I was the bad seed that would call out in the middle of class, distracting the other students. Oh, how they would laugh when I commented on a teacher's clothes, or just shout out random phrases that meant absolutely nothing. It earned me popularity, and I played up to it.

Even though inside, I was worried to death about what was happening to me. It wasn't until my older cousin Simone and I went away to our grandmothers for the weekend that the true extent of my quirks came to light. Nothing screams issues like a 12-year-old launching a rolling pin in the air and giving her Nanna a black eye.

It took months of doctors' appointments, hospital visits, specialist referrals and counselling before they finally came back with the verdict. I had Tourette's Syndrome. Deal with it.

My parents were livid. They blamed the school for not picking up on it. I'll never forget the day my dad stormed into the school, my fresh 'Statement of Needs' in his hand, and basically tore the headmaster a new arsehole. The accusations had been horrifying and embarrassing and did nothing at all to help me keep calm.

Instead of talking about what my family would like from the school in the form of support, my afro-Caribbean descended father (who was from Brixton for god's sake) had screamed racism. Never, not once had I ever been the victim of any racial slur in this school, or within any part of the community. The fact that I was mixed race had never even been in the equation. In fact, the only comments I ever received were complimentary on my black silky hair and seemingly perfect all year tan.

But it did the job. Not wanting to deal with the fallout from discrimination, my school pulled out all the stops to help me. I was assigned a teaching assistant to sit with me throughout every class, right the way through until I sat my exams in year 11. Big plus for my schooling, huge minus for my social life.

I became the special needs kid. The one that everybody smiled at and were pleasant too, but the invites to parties and offers to hang out literally stopped overnight. I was miserable.

My parents insisted that I be medicated in a bid to cure my disability and make me 'normal'. Didn't matter how much my aunt and uncle, my cousins, my nanna or I told them that I was normal, just quirky. Sometimes the doses were too much, and I would fall into something like catatonia, no tics but sadly no personality either. My parents seemed to like this the most.

They were embarrassed by my condition. I heard them at night, talking about how all this was affecting them. How people were viewing them differently. It was at that point that I realised they weren't interested in what this was doing to me, they just wanted to make it go away... for them.

If it hadn't been for Simone and Nanna, I don't know what kind of condition I would be in now. I moved into Nanna's at the tender age of 14 and never looked back.

Here I was at the grand old age of 27 and I had learned a thing or two. I had grown out of a lot of the more annoying tics, granted it had been later than what was considered normal, but I was grateful for it. Nobody wants to see a grown woman gnashing her teeth on the bus, or for that matter randomly biting her own arm. I still had scars for that one.

There were some things that I still did regularly, and no amount of medication would have altered that. I still kicked my bedroom doorframe every morning and told it, "Well don't just stand there!"

I still had triggers. Certain words or actions would prompt a tic to appear. These weren't always easy to avoid but luckily not as frequent as you might think.

I was controlled at work, always had been and very little slipped past that control. Up until today.

With a groan, I dropped my face into my palms and cursed everything. This was all totally his fault of course. You couldn't just walk around, disarming people with those bloody eyes. I mean, I bet I wasn't the only person affected by him. They just had the luxury of a working brain filter.

"Gobblecock," whispered past my lips, startling the crap out of me and causing a deep laugh to boom out from the other side of the toilet door.

I froze, my whole body locking and a torrent of pain slamming into me as my entire being screamed with the need to react. I held my breath and counted silently in my head, praying for a damn miracle that my new boss wasn't standing in the ladies' toilets waiting for me.

"Shit, sorry Will," Owen called quickly, knocking on the stall door. "I just wanted to come and check that you were ok."

Relief, unadulterated, hit my nervous system and I calmed somewhat. Reaching out, I flipped the lock over and pulled the door towards me.

"On a scale of two to ten, how bad was it?"

He dropped down on his haunches and took my hands in his. "I swear to you, it was only the bosses that heard anything. If I hadn't been standing directly behind Nicole at the time, I wouldn't have heard either. You didn't shout it."

"Are you sure?"

He gave a series of nods, amusement shining in his eyes. "Yeah, you actually said it quite conversationally. He had to ask Simone what had just happened because he thought he heard you wrong."

My mood lifted. "What did she say? Did she cover for me?"

His eyebrows drew together. "No Will, you know she can't do that. She just said that perhaps it was time for him to review the profiles on his team and lead him into her office. They've been in there ever since."

Screwing my face up, I gave him a reluctant head nod and stood from my seat on the throne. I knew he needed to be aware, although legally I didn't need to tell anyone if it didn't affect my job. I just preferred to be up front about things.

At least that had been how it was in the past. I didn't really know how I felt about him seeing my flaws.

"So... I'm interested to know how your giblets are doing. Do they still need nibbling?"

"Fuck off," I laughed, slapping him across the head and heading to the door.

"Seriously, because if this is going to be an issue for you, I know a guy that has a thing for..."

"Oh my god. Stop," I laughed, walking down the corridor, feeling much lighter than I had moments before.

Just as I was about to head back to my desk, I glanced up and caught those deep brown eyes staring at me from the open office door. He wasn't smiling but he wasn't shooting me death glares either. In fact, if I was to hazard a guess, he looked intrigued.

Gulping softly, I took my seat and tried to throw myself back into the zone, doing everything to convince myself that it was all going to be fine... as long as I didn't have to look at him.

How hard could that be?

4 – She said what now?

Perry

My day was getting stranger by the second.

Nicole was still talking to me, introducing me to my new team but all I could think about was the raven-haired beauty that had just knocked me completely off my feet. One minute I had been walking towards what could only be described as perfection. From the side, I was gifted the sight of curves that went on for days, black shiny hair that flowed about her shoulders in waves and those heels... my cock was a happy boy.

Then she turned back to her pc and I nearly stumbled. Her skin was like caramel. Even from a distance I could tell it would be smooth to the touch. And boy did I want to touch. Her cheekbones were high, her lips so damn full and pouty... I was in so much trouble.

I wasn't sure what the deal was with office romances, but I was going to find out because there was no way I was going to be able to stop myself from getting to know this woman.

Shallow? Maybe... but I also wasn't stupid. No matter how she looked, I didn't get involved with nasty or crazy. If I wanted that in my life, I would let my mother have her way and set me up.

As we'd approached the gorgeous woman, a strange case of nerves had hit me straight in the feels. I wasn't used to feeling off my game. I was far from a lady's man, but I had game. I never shied away from women, I loved the thrill of the chase. This wasn't a night out though, this was normal life and my usual tactics weren't going to work.

I pulled myself out of my head and focused on the lady in front of me as she lifted her head. Intelligent amber eyes locked onto mine and my breath caught. Like she needed another feature to get me all hot and bothered.

Get it together man!

Her much smaller hand slid into mine and an electric current seemed to flow into my veins. What the hell was happening?

Then she opened her mouth... and I nearly choked.

Before I could recover from the shock she was off and running out of the office at a speed I didn't think could be safe in those heels. Nicole mumbled something about reading the employee files and then completely changed the subject leaving me so confused it was a wonder there wasn't a giant question mark above my head.

What had just happened?

The files were useless. Nicole had waddled off to deal with a few last-minute HR issues for her maternity leave and I was doing some stalking. Willow was a model employee, smart as hell and a huge asset to this department. She'd been working here since the beginning of last year and everyone had nothing but praise for her. Her last evaluation had scored top marks, the highest in the whole department.

But apart from that, I had nothing. Except

for a cryptic comment about health issues from Nicole. I was beginning to think I'd imagined the whole comment.

Resigned to carry on investigating later, I put her file to one side and settled back in my seat. Movement out in the central office caught my eye and there she was, walking back to her desk with Owen and sporting a massive grin. Our gazes locked for a second and she quickly looked away. I felt a frown crease my brow and an uncomfortable thought took root. Was she playing me?

The more I watched her, the more convinced I became. She was good, I had to give her that. She showed no signs of struggling with her work, if anything she seemed the most focused person out there. Surely if she had issues, it would be obvious to the eye.

No, I concluded, what had happened earlier was indeed an attempt to mock the new guy. Maybe an attempt at making me feel small. Maybe she had wanted the position for herself and wanted to show me who was boss from day one. It wouldn't be the first time I'd had to put up with opposition in the workplace and I'd be damned if some cocky bitch was going to make me feel out of place.

Determined to gain the upper hand, I cracked open the info on the new multi-million-pound account that was taking precedent in the company and immersed myself in the file. I had to admit, the specs for the new phone and tablet line were more than simply impressive. The mock-ups for the account were mind blowing. Of course, when I looked at who the designer was, I had to stifle a groan.

I was going to have to work extremely closely with whoever was leading the team so of course it had to be the one woman who was trying to send my life into a whirlwind. Although, I thought with a smirk, this would give me the upper hand.

I was after all, the boss.

5 – I have a word for you...

Willow

It was mid-afternoon and only a handful of us were left in the office. Nicole had operated an early leave schedule for our team, knowing how much people loved to get away before the traffic on a Friday. So, each week, a skeleton staff would work until 5pm, whereas the rest of the staff would enjoy half hour lunches for the week and take the time as toil. It was a win win situation, happy employees, productivity remained high. It was just one of the many things we were hoping as a department Mr Moore would keep in place.

Nicole walked over to my empty side of the room and parked her bum on the corner of my desk, careful not to disrupt anything.

"One of these days you might have to organise this desk you know."

"Not in this lifetime," I quipped, leaning back in my chair and offering her an uneasy smile.

She frowned and reached for my hand. "You ok?"

"Don't really have any choice, do I? It is what it is, I'll deal with it. Besides, it's not like it's the first time I've embarrassed myself."

Her eyes searched mine as she slowly shook her head. "I know that. I just don't like it happening here, especially when I can count on this hand the number of episodes I've witnessed within these walls. This is usually a safe place for you. That worried me today."

Me too, I wanted to scream but one look at the lines of concern etched across Nicole's face had me stopping myself. She had enough to deal with. She had an hour at most left then she would be gone for months. This was meant to be a happy time for her, and there was no way I was going to be a burden.

"I don't know what that was. I think I was just startled by him. I wasn't expecting someone so..."

"Handsome?" she supplied with a grin.

"Intense." I stressed, not allowing her to get any bloody ideas in her head. But oh god yes, handsome, sexy, brooding...

"Are you listening to me?"

"Sorry, yes," I stammered, dragging my wayward thoughts back to the present.

"He's a decent man, comes highly recommended and is actually a good friend of Annie's."

Well this was news, and not the welcome sort. Annie is best friends with the big boss Jasmine Hope. Jasmine is married to Ben Hope. Ben is brother to Daniel Hope... and Daniel is married to my cousin. It's not like I didn't see these people outside of work, I saw them all the bloody time.

What were the odds?

"I just thought it would put your mind at ease, knowing that there is a connection. I know how close you have all become, Jasmine and Annie think of you like a younger sister. They wouldn't put someone in here that would be bad for the team, I assure you."

No, not for the team, but frickin bad for my state of mind.

"Anyway," she continued, completely oblivious to the battleground raging full force inside my head and wracking my body. "He wants to talk to you, clear the air. I'm going to head off home now."

She winced as she stood and began rubbing her back again. I immediately flew to my feet and started fussing around her.

"Are you ok? Do you want me to call Karl?"

"No, don't be silly," she waved me off. "Karl is home with the kids, and it takes me all of twenty minutes to get home. I'm gonna be fine."

She turned and pulled me into a hug. "I'm going to miss seeing you every day."

"You'll be too busy changing shitty nappies to miss me."

She laughed and shrugged, knowing how true it was but not really caring. My hand snapped out and rubbed against her belly again. She tilted her head to the side and smiled. "What's going to replace this tic when I'm gone?"

I smiled sheepishly. "This isn't a tic, I just let you think that. This is plain and simple, a woman being broody."

We hugged once more and then she was off, saying her goodbyes to the few of her team that were left. Owen helped her with all her gifts and flowers and the silence left in the office once the elevator door shut behind them was deafening. I hadn't realised before just how much of a safety net she was to me. A hollow feeling was taking root in my stomach, one that annoyed me more than anything. I wasn't a child. I was an independent woman. I didn't need a safety net.

My phone rang on the desk, jarring me from my thoughts.

"Marketing, Willow Summers speaking."

"Willow, could you come to my office please."

That voice. It was pure sexual confidence all wrapped up in a soothing bow of decadent power.

"Be right in," I replied calmly, replacing the phone in its cradle and silently congratulating myself for a job well done.

You got this, I repeated in my head as I walked towards the front of the room, eyes focused on the closed office door and of course, making sure I didn't trip because honestly, a girl could only take so much humiliation in one day.

"Come in Willow," he called before I had a chance to knock. I paused for a moment, strangely annoyed that he couldn't wait the two seconds it would have taken for me to rap my knuckles against the door.

Jesus, I silently berated myself. Way to throw an internal paddy about bugger all. He just made me so... unhinged, and I didn't really understand why. Yes, he was attractive. Yes, he had hypnotic eyes and a voice like the smoothest whisky.

But really that was no excuse for;

A, acting like a freak or B, acting like a fangirl.

I walked into that office with my head held high, eyes focused on the desk instead of the handsome man sitting behind it, determined to show him that I was a professional. Which would have been the case had I not put one hand on the chair to pull it out and told it, "That's a moist bird right there."

Addition to my list...

C, saying moist in any way that doesn't

involve cake.

To his credit, he didn't comment on my slip and I wasn't going to bring it up, so we sat in an uncomfortable silence for what felt like an hour but, was only a few seconds.

"You don't do it all the time then."

My eyes snapped to his, the urge to retort hot on my tongue but I managed to keep it in check.

"No, I don't."

He appraised me with those deep pools, the colour so dark they almost appeared black. Now that I was looking at him for longer than a few heartbeats, I could really take him in. Gorgeous didn't even begin to cover it. His hair was deep brown, a glorious shade of chestnut that was artfully styled. He was dressed to perfection in his three-piece suit, yet you could see he was well defined beneath the layers.

Strike that, I thought as he slipped out of his jacket and draped it over the back of his chair. The man was ripped. He rolled the sleeves up on his crisp white shirt revealing the strong contours of his forearms. He was... perfection.

"I thought now would be an appropriate time for you to explain to me why you think the lead role on the Gold Tech account would benefit from your input."

A sense of dread began to unfurl in the pit of my tummy. "Excuse me?"

He smiled without humour. "I didn't note any hearing problems in your profile Miss Summers."

"Nienawidze cie," I blurted, my eyes widening for a second.

"What was that?"

41

I waved a hand absently and tried to brush off the fact I had just told my boss *'I hate you'* in Polish, all the while reeling from the knowledge that he was in fact questioning my submission for the very account I had been working tirelessly on for months.

"My apologies Mr Moore. The reason I believe that I would benefit this account is proven in the work already done. Which I might add has already acquired praise and approval from Mrs Hope."

He leaned back in his chair, the picture of ease as he stroked a hand over his neatly trimmed beard. "I'm not questioning the mock-ups. They are certainly high quality and I commend your vision. My doubt stems from the fact that there will be a lot of presentation work involved in this account. We have had two encounters so far. Both times your... *disability*, has been affected."

It took me a few moments to process where this conversation was going but the second it did, any attraction I felt for the man went flying out the window.

"I think you'll find Mr Moore," I declared, standing abruptly from the chair and leaning onto the desk in front of me. "This company has a zero-tolerance policy when it comes to discrimination."

With that I stalked over to the door, knowing that if I stayed in his presence for a second longer something awful would happen. This man had seen enough of my weakness for one day.

"I'll see you Monday morning Willow."

"Pieprze cie," I yelled and walked as fast as I

could before I said anything else incriminating. Although, *'Fuck you'* was pretty apt...

Could this day get any worse?

6 – Polish cussing is my thang

Willow

My little one-bedroom flat was more than just my safe haven. If these walls could talk, they would narrate one hell of a bestseller. I would like to say it would be a hot and heavy romance, maybe even an intriguing life story. Alas no, it would be a comedy.

The second my feet crossed the threshold, my bag and coat hung up on the hook and my shoes neatly put away in the shoe rack... that was when the day would finally catch up with me.

It was almost like a ritual. First, I would tell my Spider plant how nice his hair looked. He never thanked me.

Then I would go about fixing something to eat, all the while compensating for the fact that my right shoulder needed to dance a little jig, shrugging up and down roughly seven times every minute. I had taught myself to be ambidextrous several years ago for this very reason.

It didn't end there. It was usually at this point that the fridge would need a good talking too about the correct way to slice a chicken breast, usually accompanied by a round of jazz hands that would get me the starring role in any Broadway musical.

Hilarious, right?

Wrong.

Because what nobody outside of this condition understood was that all these funny quirks... they hurt. Repressing the need to tic during working hours was something I was very fortunate to be able to control. My Tourette's was mild compared to others and I was grateful every day for that. But it came at a price. By the time I left the office every day my body was aching from being held so tightly together. More often than not, I would have a blinding headache too.

Imagine that being your reality, day in and day out.

It wasn't until I was home and starting to relax that the onslaught would happen. Why this triggered, I had no idea, but it was one of the reasons I hadn't ever sought out a roommate or allowed a relationship to progress very far. It was an awful lot to cope with even for me, the last thing I needed was another person watching the whole ordeal.

Back when I lived with my Nanna, she would make herself scarce until the worst of it was over. Not for her sake, but for mine. Simone didn't bat an eyelid when I acted up in front of her, but she'd had a long time to get used to it. I had friends, but even they weren't privy to my worst moments, and I made sure it stayed that way.

Tonight, seemed worse than usual, and I knew why. If being relaxed brought the tics out to play, it was nothing compared to anxiety and anger. They were the worst emotions for me and right now, with the day I had, I was suffering.

So was my doorframe.

After the third kick to the wood, and some creative phrases shouted at it, I opted to put on my walking boots just in case. Broken toes were no fun, hence why I had a rugged pair just for inside the apartment.

Glass of wine in hand (plastic cup because it was one of *those* days), I dropped onto my huge two-seater settee and sighed with relief.

Why had Perry Moore walked into my life now? I was doing so well at work, finally feeling like I had a chance to prove what I could do and along he came with his perfect hair and stupid mesmerising eyes and completely turned my universe on its head. The worst part was, the insinuation he implied that I wouldn't make a very good sales pitcher was everything I was worried about.

I knew the chances of making a fool of myself in a meeting were high, just as I knew that if I became flustered for any reason and did lose control, I could ruin the pitch all together. I didn't need some corporate arsehole telling me any of this.

But coming from him had made it seem so much worse. He may not have said the words, but I could see the future clearly and I had a bad feeling it was going to end with my ideas being pitched by one of my colleagues.

A tear slipped down from the corner of my eye, one that had no business falling when I was trying to hold onto my anger.

The phone chose that moment to ring, startling me from my pity party for one. It could only be my cousin and she was going to know from my voice that I was upset. But if I didn't answer, she would make her husband Daniel come around and I didn't have the energy for his crazy ass tonight.

"So, my new jeans arrived and the bastards don't fit," Simone exclaimed before I even had a chance to say hello.

"So, send them back."

"Uh, yeah right," she laughed. "Like I didn't think of that!"

My eyes were already rolling in my head and she'd barely been on the phone a minute. This was what she did. She didn't want to actively seem like she was checking up on me, so she would ring up to tell me random useless shit as an excuse. I loved her to pieces, but she drove me crazy.

"So, how was your day?"

"Well," I sighed. "I grabbed a dude and flicked his face in the coffee shop this morning. That was pretty epic as far as Friday mornings go. Then I met my new boss."

"Oh, we'll come back to the face flicking in a minute. What was the new guy like?"

Handsome, sexy, edible... an arsehole...

"I told him to take a knee and nibble my giblets."

Silence.

"Then later, when he upset me, I swore at him."

"In polish?"

I snorted. "Is there any other way for me?"

She laughed sharply and then sighed. "Fucking Gosia has a lot to answer for."

She wasn't wrong there. Nanna had a Polish hairdresser that used to come to the house once a week. She had a beautifully long name that none of us could pronounce, therefore we all called her Gosia. She was young and gorgeous... and swore like a sailor. Each time she did, she would turn and wink at us girls, then repeat what she had said in English. You show me a kid that wouldn't pick that shit up. It was the only thing British people were interested in when it came to learning a new language – the swear words.

My convoluted brain had kept those words all these years and I suppose I should be grateful because whenever obscenities filtered through against my will they were always, *always* in polish.

"What did you say to him?"

"I told him I hated him."

"That's not so bad, right?"

I chewed on my lip and attempted to change the subject, but my cousin knew me better than anyone.

"What else? I know there's more Willow..."

"I may have said fuck you..."

"Oh shit," she laughed quietly. "How did that go down?"

"Oh, he loved it, begged me to do it again."

"Don't get cocky," she scolded.

"Look, it's not like he knows polish! And he pissed me off, ok? He insinuated that my syndrome would hinder my ability to lead the Gold Tech project and I..."

"Oh. No. He. Fucking. Didn't."

Well, this wasn't good. Epic fail on my brain to mouth filter.

"It's fine, I'm going to show him..."

"I'm ringing Jasmine!"

"No," I shouted, alarm ringing through my ears.

"Fine! Then I'm calling Ben."

"Simone, would you just let me..."

"How fucking *dare* he, that's discrimination! I'll have his fucking head for this," she must have held the phone away from her ear because she screamed for Daniel and that was when the panic really started to set in.

I could hear her rambling away, her agitation plain as she ranted to her husband. Why the hell had I told her that last part? I knew how she would react, this was going to get messy if I didn't do something now.

"Daniel's coming over right now. You're going to sit down with him and tell him everything, and I do fucking mean everything Willow."

"Yes mum."

"Don't act like a child!"

"Don't treat me like a child then! I know this situation sucks but I will handle it myself, ok?"

She didn't answer, but then I knew she wouldn't. It wasn't in Simone's genetic makeup to back down when it came to protecting those that she loved. I had no choice but to wait for Daniel and hope I could get him to talk some sense into her.

"He's a *Dupek*," she muttered.

"Yep," I laughed. "A complete and utter arsehole."

"Make sure you call him that when you next see him."

I groaned and settled back against the cushions. "My plan is to *not* lose it Simone."

"Call him that anyway."

Laughing, I agreed with her and quickly turned the conversation round to Simone's gorgeous little girls. This was far from over, I knew that but for now we'd put a pin in it. And when my self-appointed big brother finally got here, I would convince him that there was nothing to worry about. Problem solved.

7 – Get into the groove

Willow

"I'm gonna kick his fucking arse!"

I tried really hard not to roll my eyes, I swear I did. But Daniel had been pacing the floor in my cosy living room for the last 20 minutes and quite frankly – I was bored.

"Ok I get it, you're pissed off."

He stopped and glared at me as if I was the one in the wrong here.

"This isn't funny Willow. Jasmine will fire his arse in a heartbeat once I tell her. He can't talk to you like that."

It didn't seem to matter what I said, he wasn't listening. I knew Mr Moore had been a wanker earlier, but I didn't want to be the girl who played on her disability. Not that I would dissuade someone else in my position, far from it. But something in me wanted to prove myself without running to the big boss.

"I do have a plan, you know, if you could stop wearing my carpet out for a minute and listen."

He rubbed his hands over his face and threw himself back in my easy chair. "Fine, let's hear your brilliant plan."

I eyed him suspiciously. "You're going to listen?"

"Of course," he muttered impatiently.

My eyes narrowed further but he simply waved a hand in a *get on with it* gesture.

"I need to prove that I would be the best option for this project and the only way for me to do that is do a presentation for him. I have all the mock-ups done already, all the planning is in place and has been for a while now. I just need to show him that I can face down a boardroom full of people and not fall to pieces."

His mouth flapped open uselessly. "That's it? That's your brilliant plan?"

"What's wrong with it?"

"That isn't a plan, that's you justifying what is probably already going to happen as if it's your idea."

Dammit, I had hoped Daniel was too keyed up to notice that little flaw. Truth was, I had nothing. I had thought the prep work was done with now that I had been given the lead on this project, but obviously I was going to have put myself back through the ringer. Or more to the point, *he* was going to. *Bastard.*

"What you need to do is get your tics under control around him."

Scowling, I lifted my mug of tea to my lips and refrained from poking my tongue out at him. "Wish I'd thought of that."

"Don't get cocky," he grumbled.

We sat in silence, me pouting into my drink and him drumming his fingers against the arm of the chair. He was right of course. All I really needed to do was control myself around him, the rest I could do, I just knew it. I thought back to the way he had disarmed me. Maybe, the more I was around him the easier it would be. The attraction had dimmed the second he opened his mouth and judgement flew out, so I wouldn't have to contend with that emotion anymore. Hopefully.

Eh, who was I kidding. He was still the most devastatingly gorgeous specimen I had ever laid eyes on. Just thinking about those muscles when he rolled his sleeves up had me thinking all sorts of dirty thoughts.

But it wasn't just that. It was the way he had looked at me. He'd been focused, those eyes probing deep into the very heart of me. That had been the problem in the first place. Being the centre of attention wasn't my favourite thing in the world, hence the anxiety that kicked everything off.

With a shrinking feeling, I realised that his intensity may very well be the reason I failed. He made an imposing figure, one I was going to have to deal with every day. Oh god, this suddenly wasn't just about the project, but getting through the day. Every bloody day.

And then I had a lightbulb moment.

"You're right." I glanced up to find Daniel looking at me thoughtfully. "What I need is to get comfortable in the lime light, right? Be the sole focus of a ton of eyes."

I could see his mind racing, but he didn't have a clue where I was going with it. "Well yeah, we covered that already, didn't we?"

I kept a wide-eyed look on my face and kept slowly nodding my head, waiting for the penny to drop.

"Oh, hell fucking no!" He jumped up and started pacing the floor again. "Once! You promised me it would be once. I can't take the pressure Willow."

"Pfft, what pressure? I'm the one that does all the hard work!"

He stopped and sent another of those hilarious, withering looks in my direction. "My balls. Stop being so selfish and think of my balls!"

"Ewww," I snickered. "I would rather not!"

His middle finger shot into the air and waggled in my general direction as he mumbled about bitches being crazy and how his balls would never forgive him. It didn't matter. I had a plan, one that had worked for me before and I had every reason to believe it would work again. One where I would be able to get my head on straight, face my fears and hope that the sensation lingered for a little while, just like last time.

"It helped me when I pitched to Nicole and Jasmine..."

"Shhhh I'm thinking."

I sat back in my seat and let the poor man work out his thoughts, trying not to bounce with glee the whole time. Finally, he dropped down on the sofa next to me and closed his eyes.

"I swear to everything that's holy, if Simone finds out about this and my sex life suffers, you will pay."

My hand shot into the air and pumped frantically as I squealed happily. His eyes followed the movement and turned concerned for a moment before settling back on my face.

"You sure about this?"

"If I can handle 50 pairs of eyes watching me, I can definitely cope with one pair."

He rubbed his hands down his face and gave a small nod. "Ok, fine. But you know, there's no guarantee this will work."

"It will," I plucked his phone from his pocket and placed it in his hand. "Call Mr. E."

He sighed but hit the buttons and made the call, all the while looking like he was signing his own death warrant. He wasn't of course, it had been kept a secret last time, and this time would be no different.

Tomorrow night, I would take the stage at Hot Steppers... and hoped to god it worked.

8 – I put a spell on you

Willow

"Oh, what I would give to have your hair, Willow."

I grinned in the mirror as Jezebel primped and fussed with my black locks. It didn't take much to bring the crazy curls, ala Beyoncé to the surface but this amazing man managed to make them stand out in a way I had never managed to achieve.

The DO was huge!

"Well, I think I have some to spare… How the hell do you manage to make it so…. Big?"

He just laughed and tapped the side of his nose, the same reaction he gave me the last time. I glanced to his workspace and saw a mountain of sprays, pots and tubes, all of which were blank and colour coded. I had no idea if he bought them and took the labels off, or if maybe he made his own. And he was keeping quiet either way.

Once he was finished I sat and stared at the masterpiece he had created. It was just incredible. I had never looked so polished. My hair stood out from my face in a soft afro that would make Diana Ross envious. The curls were so perfectly formed, something that I had never managed to do myself but that wasn't the only change. He had worked wonders on my makeup, buffing and primping my coffee coloured skin until it shined. That's when he dusted my body with glitter, not enough to make me look like carnival Barbie but just the right amount to catch the lights.

My makeup was heavy, much more so than I did in normal life. The dark eyeliner surrounding my eyes made me look sultry, and the silver eyeshadow seemed gaudy up close but from a distance gave the appearance of diamonds.

When it came to my lips, Jezebel had decided to make them as large and pouty as possible. My already full lips now looked constantly puckered, as if waiting to be kissed... or filled. I tried not to dwell on that.

But it did the trick, I was virtually unrecognizable.

The first and only other time I took to the stage, I had performed like any other Show Girl. It was all very Vegas, the song itself "Hey Big Spender" was cliché, but it did the trick. While we had been practicing that dance routine, I had been planning something else in my mind. I even went as far as to buy the costume... just in case.

Right now, I was thankful for my forward planning. Not that I had any clue that I would end up back here, I really had thought once would be more than enough.

"I really don't know if I'm horny or nauseous."

I looked over my shoulder and caught Daniel leaning against the wall with a contemplative look on his face.

"Well, I'm not gonna lie, the idea of you being horny in my presence makes *me* feel nauseous."

His face screwed up adorably. "That's fucking gross! Don't be disgusting, you're not even a girl."

"Uhh, I beg to differ," I said haughtily as I

56

pointed down to my rather large breasts. "What the hell do you call these then?"

"Well obviously you're *a* girl," he said as he rolled his eyes. "But to me you're just Willow."

Good answer, I thought to myself. I was quite happy to be just Willow.

"So, you know what you're doing then?"

"Yes."

"Are you sure? You haven't had a chance to practice this routine properly."

I groaned and pushed him out of my way so I could look in the full-length mirror. The look was everything I hoped it would be. The black patent heels I had rescued from the back of my wardrobe set off the black fishnet stockings in a way that made my average length legs look runway ready. Halfway up my thigh they stopped, the clips of my garter reaching down to attach to the tops. The extremely skimpy and might I add surprisingly comfortable thong covering my naughty bits did very little to do the job it was made for.

My eyes travelled up and a smile broke free when I latched onto my blood red bodice, the cups barely covering my nipples and doing the best they could to hold the ladies in their place.

Daniel came to stand next to me and held the jacket out for me to slip my arms through. This was one of my favourite parts of the whole costume. The fitted jacket was short in the front, barely reaching the bottom of my breasts but it streamlined down in the back, way down until the tails reached the bottom of my thighs. The smooth interior throughout caressed my skin, especially the bare flesh of my bottom.

Who would have thought this would give me

a little thrill to top it all off?

"Nearly done," Daniel whispered, doing his best to be supportive when I knew he would love nothing more than for me to change my mind and get the hell out of here. And not just to protect the future of his balls.

I placed the tall top hat on top of the crazy mass of curls I had going on, using the cleverly designed clips that Jezebel had hidden to fasten it tight. This hat was going nowhere, unless I wanted it too.

I twirled on the spot and held my arms out. "Well? What do you think?"

Daniel handed the cane to me, the last item for my routine and stepped back to take the whole look in.

"I say... you look fucking incredible. Knock 'em dead Willow."

I gave his cheek a quick kiss and moved to walk past him.

"And if anyone touches you, I'll break *their* fucking balls."

I could feel the crowd. It wasn't quite the same electric energy that pulsed around on a normal night. Ladies were far more intense and tended to come in lust fuelled parties to Hot Steppers.

But on Guys Night, it was a completely different feel. Or maybe that was just because I was taking the spotlight. There was an intensity to the much smaller crowd, a more intimate sensation as I stepped up to my marker on the centre of the stage and struck my starting pose in the dark.

I could hear the baited breathes collectively coming from the wide open space behind me and it was intoxicating. Hundreds of eyes, all trained on the very spot where a soft indigo light now highlighted my frame.

My cane was propped out to the side away from my body, my hip cocked out and my head tipping my hat. I waited, solely focused on the routine until the first strains of the piano played. With a deep breath, I slowly swung my hips just as Annie Lennox's powerful voice told the crowd... I put a spell on you.

I had this, I thought with a smile as I turned to face the nameless faces in the crowd. I poured every ounce of concentration I had into the turn of my foot, the slide of the fabric down my arms as I shucked the jacket. My arms worked just as they were meant to, fingers crooking in a seduction move and not a jazz hand in sight.

It was, empowering, the way the music commanded my body, the way *I* was in complete control of every move, every step, every second. I could feel the strain in my limbs, the tightness to each millimetre of my skin and the want etched through my muscles to tic, but my will overpowered it all.

I was soaring. I kept a steely eye on the men in front of me, never forgetting why I was here. I needed to prove to myself I could be in control of my own body under scrutiny... and this was the ultimate test.

Eyes roamed each and every part of me, probing gazes wanting to see it all. Didn't matter that I wasn't the best dancer, the best looking or hell, that there was a little too much junk in my trunk. They feasted on the sight. On me.

And I feasted on them.

With a practised ease that impressed the hell out of a watching Daniel from the wings (his mouth dropped open in shock, that never happens) I had the clips undone on my garter belt and was rolling to the side of the stage, holding my leg out for assistance. The handsome man reached out with trembling fingers and pulled the fishnet stocking from my body. My lips pressed together in a kiss and with a wink I slipped across the stage ready to bestow the same move for my other leg.

I couldn't help but feel acutely proud of myself as the song neared the end of my set. I was down to my next to nothing thong, my heels and hat, all three of which would stay on, and the corset that would be ripped off at the end. The club had a policy of giving the goods within the eyes of the law, that meant boobs were fine, vajayjays were not. And I was completely ok with this.

The powerhouse of words reached its climax just as I gripped the side of the corset and pulled it free from the Velcro fastening. It flew out into the clutching hands of the crowd, cheers and whistles reaching my ears as I bared the goods to them. I settled back into my starting pose, this time facing the front and feeling overwhelmed with accomplishment.

I hadn't put a foot wrong. Not once. I had it handled under pressure, just like I had thought. This thing with the new boss was just a glitch.

I cocked my head to the right and smiled into the crowd – and the last thing I saw before the lights went out was the shocked face of Perry Moore.

9 – Road to hell

Perry

There are two things I know for a fact in this world:

1 – There is never an excuse to wear socks with sandals.

2 – The person who gave this woman a driving licence should be publicly flogged with stinging nettles.

"Annie, seriously, it's called a brake for a reason."

"Oh my fucking god, are you always this much of a pussy?"

"Only when crazy bitches are trying to kill me on a dual carriageway!"

"Often then," she quipped as she slipped the large car into the tiniest gap imaginable. My life flashed before my eyes. I needed to get out more.

"Jesus Christ!"

She laughed. The crazy woman laughed as my breakfast threatened to make a guest appearance all over her nicely upholstered leather seats. If I'd used my head, I would have asked Jason to give me a lift while my car was at the garage.

"Annie, it's my first full day on the job. I would really like to get there without brown stains in my pants."

She threw her head back and laughed. I shook my head to clear it a little before turning to look at my chauffeur.

"Thanks for doing this Annie," I said begrudgingly. "Being without my car is like losing a limb."

She laughed and waved her hand as if to dismiss me. "Please, I like any excuse to go back into work and annoy everyone. I don't get to come into this place very often anymore, and especially without the kiddo."

She gave a little smile when she spoke of her son and I couldn't help smiling in return. Jamie was his father's son, sharing Jason's chilled out and laid-back attitude. I grinned inwardly thinking of the little girl Annie was carrying. No way were they hitting the jackpot twice. This girl was going to be all Annie, a feisty ball of sarcasm. God help the pair of them when she hit her teens.

"Besides I can't wait for you to see the big boss in action." She waggled her eyebrows. "She's a real ballbuster!"

"I thought she was meant to be your best friend?"

"Yeah, what's your point?"

"You think she's good with you making her out to be a bitch?"

"Believe me," she chuckled. "Jasmine is awesome, but in this place, she is the big Kahuna, the big boss, the one with the biggest balls. What she says goes and she plays hard ball. You can't be a female in this cut-throat business and be a soft touch.

"Yeah I can imagine that's true." My phone blipped in my jacket pocket and without even bothering to look, I silenced it. Very few people had my number, chances were I didn't want to take the call.

"Still avoiding the mother dearest?"

"Yup," I replied, popping the p and turning to

gaze out of the side window. *Bad choice*, I thought to myself as the scenery went whizzing by.

"You're gonna have to talk to them eventually," she mused.

I knew that. It wasn't that I didn't want to see them or talk to them. I loved my folks. I just didn't particularly want to get into the whole, it's time you settled down talk. Yet again.

"Is that the only thing playing on your mind? You've been quiet since yesterday.

Wasn't that the question of the week.

Saturday night was still plaguing my every thought and it pissed me off. It was meant to be a night out with some old friends to let off some steam. All I'd wanted was to have a drink, check out some hot scenery and forget about the feisty woman that had stood in my office and given me the biggest hard-on even as she dressed me down. Instead I got to see her again – in technicolour detail.

That woman was... damn. She was just perfect. Seeing her dressed like a fucking wet dream was one thing, but when the clothes came off and she was standing there, posed and pointy... my cock was still weeping for her.

Didn't change the fact that she had still been trying to psyche me out minutes before I gave her something to really think about. The way she'd reacted in my office... I had to wonder if maybe there was something I didn't know. It had been fun outing her on the spot, alluding to know what her mystery disability was but the more I had thought about it yesterday, the more I wondered if I had in fact, crossed a line.

The idea made me feel a little ill.

I didn't want to get a reputation for being an arsehole and more to the point, I knew that discrimination in any form was severely frowned upon these days. As it should be.

"Earth to frat boy," my friend cackled next to me.

"Sorry Annie." It hit me then that she knew the woman in question and could probably shed a little light on the situation. "Hey, you know Willow Summers, right?"

"Willow?" She swerved much too sharply onto the slip road and I swear I saw my life flash before my eyes. "She's awesome. Jas and I adopted her."

"She seems nice," I hedged, not wanting to cause the crazy woman in charge of the fast-moving vehicle to get angry with me. My life was hanging in the balance.

"More than just fucking nice. Anyone that can make a best friend out of Daniel Hope and completely earn his loyalty deserves a medal."

"Are they that close?"

Annie made a loud snorting sound. "He's married to Willow's cousin Simone. The girls are more like sisters though. Since the day they met, Daniel and Willow hit it off. Or so I'm told, it was way before my time obviously."

"I've met Simone. She and Willow are nothing alike."

Annie glanced over with a frown on her face. "What's with the twenty questions?"

"Dammit Annie, watch the fucking road."

"I know what this is about," she began, shaking her head. "This is because Simone is white, and Willow has a *very* healthy tan... right?"

I spluttered in response. "Don't be ridiculous! I couldn't give a shit what colour a person's skin is!"

"Calm your tits," she laughed. "I'm totally messing with you."

The car screeched to a halt just before hitting the side of the Gold Dime Groups building... I had a feeling my boxers would need changing after all.

"She has Tourette's Syndrome."

My eyes closed briefly before I addressed this new revelation. "That's the disease where people shout abuse, right?"

Annie slugged me in the shoulder and shot a look of distaste in my direction. "Don't let anyone else hear you call it a *disease* mate."

"Shit, Annie," I rubbed at my poor abused body. "I didn't mean anything by it."

"I know, but other people wouldn't."

She jumped out of the car and waited for me to join her on the path. "I'm assuming you've already had a standoff with our girl?"

"How did you guess?" I grumbled.

"Because you're all sullen and grumpy." She poked her hand through my arm. "Do yourself a favour and read up on the syndrome. Tourette's Hero dot com is a great place to start. Ok?"

I had to hand it to her, she was right. I spent most of the day researching and it was eye opening. In more ways than one.

Because A, I had grossly insulted someone with a disability all because I didn't think she *had* a disability. I wasn't sure if that made me a *stupid* arsehole or just a *complete* arsehole...

And B, I realised that Willow was neither nasty or crazy – and that, I thought while giving my very happy dick a pat, meant she was fair game!

10- No speak English

Willow

I was wound so tight it was a wonder I hadn't exploded. Every bang of a door, every time the phone rang, I was jumping a foot in the air. Now let me tell you, for someone with my condition, this was by far the worst emotional state to be in. If I was at home I'd be a mess, but here in the office... well let's just say I would be in some serious pain by the time I got home.

How I had managed to make it off the stage in one piece Saturday night was beyond me. Seeing my boss, no more than 10 feet away from me as I struck a sexy pose with my ladies on show for the world to see was by far the most surreal experience of my life. I spent the entire day Sunday alternating between moving to Alaska and convincing myself that he didn't realise it was me and was just struck dumb at my assets...

Yeah, I know. Who was I kidding.

I nearly called in sick.

I nearly came clean to Daniel about Mr Moore being there.

I very nearly rang Simone and confessed everything.

Sense had prevailed before I could finish dialling her number luckily. No need to drag Daniel's balls into my drama.

When I walked through the doors this morning, I fully expected him to be lying in wait, ready to hand me my termination letter but he was nowhere in sight. The door to his office was closed and there he stayed the entire day. It was more than a little unnerving.

The day had settled around me and I worked my arse off to complete as many outstanding projects as I could. I needed to stay on my game, just in case he tried to say I wasn't giving the company as much attention as my other pursuits. In my head, we had an endless dialogue going on, and in each one he looked at me like something he had stepped in.

But try as I might to make him out to be the bad guy, I couldn't help but feel foolish. It was my choice to go back to Hot Steppers and I couldn't blame anyone but myself for that decision. I didn't wear a mask because stupidly, I figured with the copious amounts of makeup Jezebel made me wear, I didn't think anyone would recognise me.

I had barely recognised me.

It was this thought that was going around in my mind when Owen sidled up next to my desk.

"Are you ready? I'll give you a lift home."

I looked at the files I had piled on my desk and the numerous programmes still running on my screens and gave a hefty sigh. "No, I really want to finish these last few bits. Go on without me, the walk will do me good tonight."

He eyed the clock and I could see it was on the tip of his tongue to argue with me.

"Honestly Owen, I'll be out of here by six at the latest. Go..." I made a shooing gesture, pretending to push him away.

"Ok, be careful and keep your phone on you."

"Yes sir!"

He ruffled my hair and called me a choice word before he left me alone in the office. Well not entirely alone. At some point during the last few minutes, Mr Moore's door had mysteriously opened. I could see him leaning back in his chair, eyes focused on the screen to his left. His cuffs were folded up again, showing those strong forearms and for a second I let myself be attracted to him.

Just for a second though.

My desire to work had fled right along with Owen so I began shutting down the system and straightening the files. I didn't like being alone here with him, it had all my senses on high alert and the urge to flee was getting stronger by the minute. The second the screens went dark I was on my feet, coat in hand and hot footing it towards the main door.

I was so close; my hand was on the handle ready to push it open when I heard a throat clearing behind me.

"I was hoping to catch you before you left Miss Summers. Can I have a word?"

I closed my eyes and let my forehead thunk against the glass door. "Do we have to?"

He chuckled low and deep behind me and damn if it didn't cause goosebumps to travel up my arms.

"We really do."

"Fine," I grumbled, pushing myself away and turning to stomp past him into his office.

He followed closely, the scent of his expensive aftershave lingering in the air only to intensify when I stepped through the door. He shut us in and breezed past me, his hand gesturing towards the chair. I lowered myself carefully and sat ramrod straight, working like crazy to keep my focus.

His eyes watched me, those intense brooding

eyes that looked like liquid seduction...

"I'd ride that rooster."

Kill me... kill me now.

My lips pursed, my eyes closed, and I just gave in. That was it, I was fired, I was so out of this place...

"I'm sorry."

My frown deepened. "Excuse me?"

He sighed wearily. "I owe you a huge apology. More than that really. At the time, I wasn't fully aware of your disability details, not that it should have made a difference. The way I spoke to you on Friday was so far out of line..."

"No shit Sherlock."

He laughed and rubbed his hands down his face. "Yeah, I know."

I relaxed a little in my chair and studied the man before me. He looked tired, a little dishevelled from the day but none the less impressive. He had a five-o-clock shadow that gave him a rugged look and brought all sorts of naughty ideas into my head. Now *that* I couldn't have. I had limited experience in the dating world because my mouth tended to say what it wanted long before my brain could filter it. I had been called tactless on more than one occasion, even from those that were aware I had little say on what I... um... said.

So, to be having body rocking thoughts about this man had alarm bells ringing all over me.

"Maybe it would be best if I transferred..."

"No."

I raised an eyebrow. "No?"

He looked a little out of sorts, but he rolled his eyes in his head and held a hand up. "This is awkward."

I sat back and let him have a moment because I honestly didn't have a clue what was going on in his head. After what felt like a lifetime, he groaned and leant forward on the desk.

"I judged you unfairly. Believe me when I say, I am the last person on this earth that normally behaves like that."

"Ok. Say I believe that. Why did you."

He rubbed his hands down his face in what I was beginning to suspect was a nervous gesture. "I don't want to say."

I laughed. I couldn't help it.

"Seriously Mr Big Shot? That's your defence?"

He smiled at me and I swear I heard harps playing. What the fuck was going on with me?

"I love your laugh, Miss Summers."

We both paused and locked eyes. I could feel my heart in my throat, or maybe that was nervous gas. Oh, please don't let it be gas.

"Are you hitting on me Mr Moore?"

"No, of course not," he replied smoothly. "That would be inappropriate behaviour in the workplace."

Wow, built up and knocked back down in less than 30 seconds. That was a new record for me.

"However, if we were to go and have dinner…."

And now I'd hit my limit of reading between the lines. I didn't do subtle and this was winding me up tighter than a spring.

"Look, I can't do this." I stood and gathered my bag and coat. "I don't do dates and with my track record of embarrassing myself in your presence, not only would it be the date from hell, we'd probably get banned from the restaurant."

"So, we go to my place."

Was he for real? "Why the hell would I go to your place? Do I look like a hooker?"

And when that little sparkle lit his eyes I realised that yes, he probably *did* think I was that easy. And, why wouldn't he? He'd already seen most of the goods.

"Ok arsehole, let's be real fucking clear right here. Just because you saw me stripping does not mean that I'm gonna jump on your Armani covered cock. Capish?"

He laughed, a full-on belly laugh that I absolutely refused to find sexy. Jesus, seriously, what was wrong with me. I shot him the bird and flung his door open, determined to walk away with my head held high...

"My turkey needs basting!"

...and die a slow death.

11 – Cat and Mouse

Willow

An endless cycle of awkward had slipped into my daily routine. Among the usual shit my brain and body liked to throw at me, I now had the added bonus of a new game I liked to call 'avoiding the dick'.

On Tuesday, Mr Moore had asked for me to meet with him to discuss a sports clothing line I had been working on the promo for.

I sent him the file via email and faked a very long winded phone call with the talking clock.

On Wednesday when his deputy Harry called me over to arrange for me to sit in with a conference call with the boss and one of the contracts, I deftly had the switchboard forward the call to my desk – complete accident of course.

Yesterday had been particularly clever on my behalf. I managed to switch my monthly review with another colleague so that mine was at the end of the day and then, the irony, my doctor's office called and requested I drop by the surgery. Ok that *did* actually happen but what I didn't mention was that I could have gone by this morning to collect my repeat prescription.

The Pill was hardly life or death. But it had worked in my favour, so I went with it.

Today however, I didn't think I was going to get away with it. It was my week to leave early but with the crap on my desk waiting for me, it wasn't looking likely. I glanced up and caught the boss staring intently at me, a cheeky grin on his face that had my gut clenching... along with other body parts.

I had lost count of the amount of times my libido had double crossed me this week. At night, when the lights were off and my body was chilled out, it was him that I thought about in my bed. Each time I ended up sneaking a hand into my pyjama bottoms and tapping out a tune I had no business humming.

I was attracted to him, there I said it. But I didn't want to be. He was old school, stuck up money from what I had heard and nowhere did a woman like me fit into his world. If my colour and background didn't prove it, my other situation would surely do the trick.

I wasn't sure how much he knew about my Tourette's and each time the conversation should have happened – well, it had gone horribly wrong. I didn't want to ring Nicole and ask her, she had enough to deal with now that her bouncing baby girl had been born.

So that left me up shit creek without a paddle. Or a life preserver.

I couldn't settle today either, so my work was suffering too. I had been staring at the same mock-up for the last twenty minutes and I couldn't even tell you which account it was for. With a sigh, I pushed out of my chair and stalked to the break room. Maybe a strong coffee would help me gain some focus.

As per usual, the kettle was empty, so I filled it up and stood there while it boiled, contemplating how I'd managed to find myself in such a confusing situation.

"Alone at last."

The voice jolted me out of my thoughts and before I was even aware it was happening, my head jerked back and collided with the bottom of Mr Moore's chin. He slumped backwards with an audible groan and while I wanted to apologise, I couldn't get the words out because my poor hands had taken on a life of their own, jazzing up the place.

I heard the door to the tiny kitchenette close and I leaned forward against the counter, heat prickling at the back of my eyes and morbid embarrassment hitting me square in the chest. I was so done for. I couldn't work here anymore. He was probably filing a complaint against me right now...

"Are you ok?"

Surprised to find him still here, I turned around slowly and watched as he rubbed at his chin.

"I am so, so sorr..."

"Stop!"

My mouth snapped shut as he walked over to me. When he was in reaching distance, I backed up against the counter, my breath catching in my chest in sheer panic at was he was about to say. Was he going to fire me?

"You're excused for the day. Go and get your things and wait for me in the lobby."

I opened my mouth to protest but he held up a hand, a silent command that this little game had gone on far enough. "Miss Summers, I'm asking you very nicely to do as I say. It has been a long week and my patience is at breaking point. Go. Now."

I didn't need to be told twice. Ok, well, clearly I did but I wasn't going to be told a third time. I scrambled past him as if the hounds of hell were on my tail and did exactly what he asked.

Within record time I was downstairs in the lobby, heading for the doors and with only a split-second hesitation, I was through them and out into the busy street.

One step, two steps away from the building, I stopped. He was right. For my own sanity, I couldn't carry on like this. The whole week had taken its toll on me in so many ways. While there had been a funny side to the avoidance, the other side of the coin was far from amusing.

I was exhausted. The sheer will and concentration it had taken to just survive at work this week had been paid back tenfold every night when I walked through the door at home. Sore muscles and tired eyes were just a part of the chaos, my head had been thumping more than ever. I couldn't carry on like this and if I had to say goodbye to the Gold Dime Group, then so be it.

"I thought you'd gone."

I raised my face and offered a timid smile. "This isn't going to work Mr Moore."

He shook his head and took a hold of my arm, gently steering me around to his right. By this point, I didn't even have the inclination to stop him, I just rolled with the punches.

"I think we just need to start again."

"I wouldn't even know where *to* start."

He chuckled, that deep sexy timbre that even in my tired state did something to me. "Lucky for you, I do."

✓✓✓

The cup of warm hot chocolate felt good

against my hands. His idea of a good place to talk was Lakeland Park, a well used walkers route surrounding a picturesque lake. So here we sat, right on one of the many small docks and threw bread to the ducks.

While I was still very much in turmoil, I had calmed enough to the point where I could breath.

"Can I ask you a question?"

It was the first thing he had said since we sat down. I gave him a small nod and went back to watching the lake.

"Why do I make you so on edge?"

A nervous laugh tickled the back of my throat and since I was near enough resigned to finding a new job, I thought what the hell. "It's your eyes. They're intense."

He didn't say anything to that but then, I hadn't expected him too. He was probably thinking I was weirder than he had originally thought, and I was ok with that too.

"Good intense or bad intense?"

"Does it matter?" I sighed.

"Well," he gripped the back of his neck and rubbed absently at the skin. "It would help me decide which way to take this conversation."

"Look, for whatever reason you put me on edge. I can't explain it really, so it would just be a hell of a lot easier..."

I didn't get to finish my sentence, not when I looked at him and found his lips dangerously close to mine. There it was, plain to see on his face. He was going to kiss me. No, no, no... I couldn't handle this, not from him. He was entirely too gorgeous, and breath-taking, and he was my boss! What do I do?

The answer?
I shoved my phone in his face.

12 - Memes explain everything

Willow

He hadn't said a word since he got a kisser full of my phone. He was just sitting there holding it in his hand and staring at the screen. I didn't blame him, he had gotten the shock of his life. One minute he was going in for the kill... the next he was facing a set of crazy eyes on a smartphone screen!

> *I promise this isn't a threat*
> *It won't work, I swear, no regrets*
> *I'll kick, shout and mutter*
> *Get your mind out the gutter*
> *'Coz this is my life with Tourette's*

Funny how I'd used this move on so many people, both those that were hitting on me and those that got to witness my behaviour first hand, yet for once I wished I could snatch the phone back and hit rewind.

I had made the meme after a particularly frustrating night out with my friends. I didn't usually join them on their wild nights on the town for obvious reasons, but it had been Owens birthday and he begged. Owen had been a good friend to me, long before we started working at Gold Dime together and I felt I owed it to him to show my face.

The night had been a personal disaster filled with more cheesy chat up lines than I could count. Apparently, the rest of our party had picked the venue and lapped up the attention... me, not so much.

It was hell. The place had been crammed, there were bodies swaying way too close to mine which was a trigger for me anyway but to have them invading my space on purpose – it had been more than I could cope with. The tics had been out in force and I lasted barely an hour before I bailed on the night.

I never wanted to be in such a situation again, therefore I made the screensaver and had been using it ever since. For the most part it worked, at least as far as guys on the prowl went. Little old ladies that got lectures on proper poultry etiquette however, that was a little awkward.

Now I was faced with someone that I *did* like, that was in no way a good match for me, but I desperately wanted him to be. A girl could only lie to herself so much and I was done with it. I had the hots for Perry Moore – and I had just effectively given him the brush off.

Fabulous!

"Why is it always chickens?" He finally asked.

"It isn't."

He turned his body towards me on the bench and snaked an arm along the back of it. He was close, so very close...

"I talk about all poultry. I'm an equal opportunities kinda gal."

His laugh was like music to my ears. "Ah yes. You did tell me your turkey needed basting."

My smile was small and short lived. "Just a drop in the ocean, Mr Moore."

"Perry."

"Huh?"

He reached over and pushed a loose strand of my hair behind my ear. "Please call me Perry.

Mr Moore makes me feel like the creepy boss hitting on a secretary."

It was on the tip of my tongue to remind him this was quite an accurate description, but he put a finger to my lips. "I know, ok. I haven't exactly played this very well."

My head pulled back far enough to lose the contact. I missed the touch immediately. "I don't even know what *this* is."

He sighed and shuffled a little closer on the bench. "This is by far the worst case of playground tactics ever played by a grown ass man."

He chuckled at my confused face. "The boy at school that picks on the girl, pulls her ponytail. All because he likes her and doesn't want to show it?"

"Well, that's just mean."

"Right?" He dropped his head back on his shoulders and stared at the sky. "I usually have much better game than this. I walked into the office that day and you stood right out. I don't think you realise how beautiful you are. You light up a room. I was hoping to get to know you and see if there was a chance... and then you threw me completely for a loop."

I cringed a little, thinking on the giblets quote but said nothing. I could apologise until I was blue in the face, but it wouldn't change anything. I *couldn't* change anything and if Perry was interested in me, it was something he was going to have to come to terms with.

"Nicole was tight lipped and merely said you had some health issues and that I should get myself up to speed with my staff. Which would have been a damn sight easier if there was something in your profile about it. But there wasn't..."

A frown creased my forehead but still I didn't speak. I assumed it was all on record, it wasn't something I had hidden from Nicole or Jasmine. They had obviously deemed it *need to know.*

"Then I thought that maybe, it was a joke you were playing on the new guy. Which pissed me off because, well... I was crushing."

"You were?" Dammit, I hadn't meant to ask that. He smiled softly and turned to look at me again.

"I still am."

Oh, the fluttering. A pack of excited butterflies had spawned inside my tummy. I felt sick with anticipation as he leaned forward once again, knowing that I wasn't going to back away this time. His scent drew me closer and for once, just once, I wanted this to be perfect. For my moment to happen...

Firm, full lips pressed against my own, gentle at first, as if this small piece of time could shatter at any moment. My breath caught for precious seconds, every nerve in my body straining to deepen the kiss. He pulled back and gazed at me in shock.

"Fucking hell," he whispered before lowering his lips back to mine, this time a little harder.

I melted. There was nothing but me and Perry, two souls smouldering with the simmering passion of a new attraction burning between us. My poor brain was overheating with romantic prose and simpering analogies but right now, I didn't care.

Because Willow Summers was having one hell of a moment and nothing would ruin it...

"Stuff that bird good and proper, don't be shy."

… and back to reality.

✔✔✔

"So, I'm a little confused. You insulted your boss, and then he kissed you."

"It was a little bit more than that…"

"Shut up, I'm trying to understand."

I grabbed a can of Pepsi Max from the fridge and tried not to groan into the phone. "I've explained like three times now Simone."

"Humour me. He was a jerk, you argued, he was a jerk again… you nutted him in the chin. Then, he takes you to the park, kisses you… and now he's coming over for dinner?"

Well when she put it like that, it sounded mental. "Basically, yeah."

"Are you fucking insane!"

There it was. Overprotective cousin alert. Of course, from her point of view it was severely fucked up. Maybe not even just from her point of view. I didn't know what the hell I was doing, but when I tried to do a runner after I messed up our epic first kiss, he had convinced me to have dinner with him tonight. I wasn't ready for a date as such and there was no way I was going to his place until we addressed the whole stripping thing that had somehow been brushed under the carpet. So, he was coming here which was both a blessing and a curse.

Great, because I was more relaxed in my own surroundings and felt safe. Bad because I was more relaxed in my own surroundings… and that meant tic central.

My ritual crazy hour was over thankfully but that didn't change the fact that at home, I didn't try to suppress myself. And I wasn't about to start now. In the back of my mind I knew I was setting us up to fail, or maybe I was just hoping he would be able to deal.

"I'm coming over," she grumbled in my ear, catching my attention.

"No, you're not."

"Oh yes I am girl."

"Simone?"

"What?"

"I love you."

She paused for a moment. "I love you too."

"I know. So please understand when I tell you that if you or your husband come around here tonight, I will disown both your arses."

She snorted down the phone. "Not the first time you've threatened something like that."

"Well this time I mean it. I really like this guy. I think he likes me too. I have no clue how things have turned around like this, but I want to see what happens."

Complete silence greets my rant and while I'm concerned because Simone doesn't usually know how to be quiet, I take the opportunity to close the deal.

"I have you guys on speed dial. But he's my boss, a friend of Annie's and works for Jasmine. Do you really think I'm in danger?"

"Not physically," she sighed dejectedly. "But none of them can help protect your heart."

I could hear the worry but also knew that she would honour my wishes. I finally managed to get her off the phone with a promise to call her in the morning with the details. When the doorbell rang a few minutes later, I sent up a little prayer that the gossip would be good – and poultry free.

13 – A man with two names

Willow

Gone was the business man. His swanky suits had been replaced with jeans and a black shirt that fit his amazing chest like a second skin. As he stood there in the doorway, a small smile on his face as he appraised me, I felt like I was watching this whole scene from above.

"Are we gonna eat in the hallway?"

Feeling stupid, I backed away and pushed the door open further, silently inviting him in. He placed the bag of Chinese food on my little table and shut the door behind him, while I still stood there taking him in. His hand slipped around my waist and gently coaxed my body towards his. I went willingly, obviously... who wouldn't?

His lips softly landed on mine and I was gone yet again, a slave to his tender kiss. He was a walking contradiction. He looked like the type to be demanding, to be rough but every touch between us had been careful, sweet, almost measured. I loved it, but a small part of me wanted to know if he was treading lightly for my benefit. I didn't want him to be anything other than himself. I knew what it was like to hold yourself back.

So, when maybe I should have pulled away like a lady, I pressed my body into his, flung my arms around his neck and took control.

He groaned, his hand slipping down to grab onto my arse and squeezing. A startled yelp escaped from my busy lips, but I didn't stop. My tongue slipped forward, licking along the seam of his lips and when he opened to me, I went for it. I had never been the aggressor, never wanted anyone with a relentless passion like he was bringing out in me.

The kiss deepened further and before long I found myself pinned against the wall, my legs around his narrow waist and my hands plunging through his deep chocolate locks. I could feel him against me, he was into this just as much as I was. So when I rubbed against his hard, denim covered cock, I felt it all the way to the centre of my body.

His mouth ripped away from mine, both of us gasping for breath. "Shit Willow."

Panting, I rested my head against his and tried to steady myself. "Something like that."

He laughed softly and placed another kiss against my greedy lips, this one much sweeter than the last. "We need to eat. We need to talk. Now, before I forget that I'm a gentleman."

I debated for a moment, not at all sure that I wanted him to remember he was a gentleman, but I knew he was right. This was all happening so fast and this wasn't at all how I played things. Not even remotely close.

"Fine," I grumbled, dropping my legs to the ground and missing the way he'd been pressed up against me.

The walk to the kitchen seemed like a mile with him close behind me and my libido raging like crazy. I didn't know what this man had done to me, but all I could think about was how to put my little kitchen table to good use, preferably with something other than food laid out on it. Or maybe the food too...

He helped me dish up and fetched the beers

from the fridge, ever the picture of manners. It was nice having someone in my personal space for once. Surprisingly the conversation flowed easily too. We had grown up in Reading, albeit on very different sides of the track.

"My parents have lived in the same house for years. It's great, but I wasn't a fan of the neighbourhood."

"Where was that," I asked, finding it hard to believe that he hadn't lived in splendour.

"The Warren in Caversham."

I nearly choked on my spring roll. "Shit, what a dive."

I knew he came from a family that had money about them, but I'd had no idea just how big the divide was. The Warren was the elite area of Reading, somewhere that the likes of Simone and I didn't dare to go near when we were kids. Just an apartment in that community would cost more than I would be able to earn in my lifetime.

"Yeah ok, it's a gorgeous place to live. But my parents were, still are, every inch the Stepford's. They don't like to be outdone by anyone, so it always felt like we were in competition with the neighbours. Drove me crazy."

"Better than having parents that wrote you off once they realised you were defective."

He stopped chewing and glanced at me in horror. "You're kidding!"

I sighed and put my fork down. "Not quite like that. They just weren't any good at dealing with me. I went to live with my Grandmother in my early teens and I can count on one hand the number of times I speak to them each year now. I haven't physically seen them in four years."

89

"Did they move away?" He questioned, adorably confused by the situation.

"Nope, still live in Grindley."

He opened his mouth, but this train of thought wasn't something I liked to talk about, so I cut him off.

"So, did the parentals try to marry you off? I thought their type liked to arrange 'influential marriages'."

I sniggered at my own joke but noticed his face turn into a small grimace. "Funny you should say that..."

Oh god. I rolled my eyes and went back to eating my noodles. I didn't really want to know about the perfect match his parents had for him, I was already feeling a little out of my league. The last thing I needed was the image of a perfectly coiffed Posh Barbie as my nemesis.

"Hey," he snagged my hand and brought it up to his lips. "Trust me when I say, my parents have never been able to make me do anything I didn't want to do. I even went as far to change my name on my passport and driving licence to show them I was my own person."

He rubbed my palm against the side of his face, the whiskers on his cheek making my skin tingle. I was lost to him, yet again...

"Wait, hold the phone! What was your real name?"

"I'm not saying."

"Oh, come on!"

"No way, you'll hold it against me."

"I'll just ask Annie then."

He gasped theatrically. "You wouldn't."

I laughed and jumped up from the table, running into the front room to find my mobile. I was inches away from dialling Annie when I felt his arms wrap around me from behind and spin me onto the sofa. He came down on top of me and what started as convulsive laughter while he wrestled my phone out of my hand ended on a breathless whimper when he shifted slightly, and parts of his hard body bore down directly on some soft parts of mine.

Our gazes locked and just like every time I looked into his eyes, I drowned in them. Strong fingers stroked down my cheek as his face inched nearer, my own fingers forgetting the gadget clutched in their grasp. My phone dropped to the carpet and I grasped at the firm muscles bunching in his back.

"My name," he whispered seductively. "Is Reginald Percival Moore."

Laughter belted from my lips as I died then and there on the spot. "Oh Reggie!"

He laughed and dropped his head onto my chest while I played around with this latest information. Reg, Percy, oh the quips were endless and by the time I ran out I was breathless yet again.

He raised his head along with an eyebrow. "Are you done Miss Summers?"

I smiled up into his handsome face. "Not even close."

14 – Leave a message...

Perry

I sat there watching Willow as she slept long enough that if anyone had been looking through the window, they would have thought I was a creeper. Then again, if they were looking through the window, they would have had no room to judge.

The night had been, incredible. I felt connected to the complex woman in a way I had never thought possible. She was sweet and sassy, fun and deep, innocent and yet so... damn, she was sexy. More so because she didn't even know it.

I'd had my fair share of women in the past, some of them long term, some of them fleeting. Ok, most of them fleeting. She was nothing like anyone I had ever met before. We'd covered a lot of ground tonight and my head was still spinning. I think I knew more about Willow than all my ex's put together.

I was jarred from my stalker like gazing when my phone blipped yet again. With a sigh, I looked at the screen and frowned. My mother had been ringing and texting me steadily throughout the evening and I knew I couldn't put off going to see her for much longer.

With one last lingering look at the woman who'd done a serious number on my heart, I dropped a kiss to her forehead and slipped out the door, making sure to lock it for her. My newly fixed car was cold when I jumped in, but it was nothing to how cold I felt when I started looking through my mother's texts.

It's been nearly two weeks Reginald...

Most children like visiting their parents...

Do I need to visit Stephanie's? Because if that's what it takes, I will...

Oh shit, Annie would shit a brick if my mother turned up at her house. It was just past ten, so I fired off a quick text thinking she would be in bed, only to have her name flash up almost the second it was delivered.

I groaned and considered throwing the bloody thing out the window but the threat of her in the same room as my friend had me pulling up my big boy pants and hitting the button.

"Evening mum."

"Good god Reginald, the lengths I have to go to just to get a greeting from you?"

That was a new record I thought with a smirk. *Good god, Reginald* was usually thrown at me a little further into the conversation. My skills were obviously improving.

"Been busy mum, starting a new job and looking for a house. You know how these things go."

She harrumphed down the phone daintily. "I most certainly do not know how these things go. You could have come here rather than bunking down with *that girl.*"

Another record! Annie bashing was another of the usual berating topics, I was definitely on a roll.

"Was there something you wanted?"

"As a matter of fact, yes."

I knew it. For her to be this persistent, she wanted something, and I was positive I wouldn't like it.

"I'm sure you realise it's mine and your

father's wedding anniversary in a few weeks," she began and to save more bellyaching on her part, I made a small agreeable sound. "We've decided to throw a party, nothing elaborate, just a few friends and family of course."

Wait for it…. Wait for it…

"No more than 100 guests…"

There it is! My mother didn't do small and intimate. "Sounds great."

"Well of course," she sniffled haughtily.

I put the car in drive and switched her to the Bluetooth, rolling my eyes when her stuffy voice echoed through the car. She hadn't always been so set in her ways. I remembered a time when she would laugh genuinely, when she would go without makeup, just for a few hours and bake with my brother and I in the kitchen. Money had never been much of an issue, so she had been a stay at home mum when we were growing up. They were good memories. Then my dad got a huge promotion within the solicitors he worked for, made partner and from there we went from being financially comfortable to a whole new level. Their attitude had changed overnight. They hosted parties for entitled clients and made my brother and I dress the part. We already had ridiculous names, ridiculous clothes weren't going to make much of a difference.

Baking days were forgotten while she made a name for herself in the social circles of the well to do. Her sense of humour seemed to be forgotten too. She still showed us love, still hugged us and kissed us and always without fail, put us to bed at night, but as for family time? That was something of a public event.

I remember my 14th birthday like it was yesterday. All I wanted to do was have some time with my family, then go out and see my friends like any other teenager. What I ended up with was a posh restaurant with my dad's business partners and a single candle put in some fancy dessert I couldn't even pronounce.

Epic!

And she had hated Annie right from the word go. That dreadful girl wasn't allowed anywhere near my house. According to my parents, she was gold digging. Why they would think that about a girl of 12 is still a mystery.

She even accused Annie of trying to sleep with me to get herself pregnant. The thought still made me gag. Now that Annie was a happily married woman however, she was acceptable. More or less.

My mother was insane.

"I've arranged a date for you already, since you're still so desperately single."

"Whoa, wait a minute! That is *not* happening."

"Oh yes it is, young man! I can't have you parading around here on your own, what would the neighbours say?"

"Jesus Christ mother," I laughed without humour and pulled into Annie's driveway. "Three guesses who you're trying to set me up with again."

"Don't be like that, she's a lovely girl. I've already made sure she's available for the evening..."

"I have a girlfriend..." I blurted, my eyes widening in shock in the rear-view mirror.

Silence followed, and I scrambled for

something to say to get me out of this.

"A girlfriend?"

"Ummm... it's still new, but yes."

Silence again. This was new. I put the phone back to my ear and locked up, waiting for her to say something and yet she was still silent.

"Are you still there?"

"Yes, of course," she stuttered. "What is this new lady friend of yours called?"

I walked through the front door and smiled as Annie and Jason tried to entertain a teething Jamie on the front room floor. "Her name is Willow."

Annie's ears perked up, but I ignored her for a moment. This conversation was way too dangerous to make a mistake.

"And you like her?"

"Yes mum," I cautiously replied. "I like her a lot."

Annie beamed at me and offered a high-five to her husband, who to his credit didn't even need to look at her to make it work. That right there was epic team work.

"Then you'll bring her to dinner tomorrow night. See you at 7pm."

What the fuck? "Wait... what...hello? Mum, are you still there?"

Oh shit!

"Oh shit, shit, shit..." I stumbled into the room and slumped down on their sofa. "Ohhhhhhh shit!"

I felt a heavy hand slap my leg. "You and Willow huh?"

I opened an eye and squinted at the large man waggling his eyebrows. "Yep."

"She's hot," he continued.

"Yep," I replied, my eyes narrowing.

Annie's hand whipped out and slapped the back of his head. He just laughed. They were a weird couple.

"I knew it. All those questions, all the broodiness this week..." she sighed.

"You mean, Jas and you have been on the phone for hours because the rumour mill at work has been going nuts." Jason rolled his eyes and turned his face to mine. "You were spotted getting hot and heavy in the park dude."

"Jason! You're a twat."

"Love you too babe."

"Are you guys serious? Is it all around work?"

She gave a small nod while still glaring at her husband... who was still waggling his eyebrows only now it was directed at her.

"Great, so now she has to contend with office gossip and a meal at my parents."

"What?" Annie practically screeched. "Why the hell would you take her there?"

"It was a fucking accident!" I yelled back.

She raised her brow, silently challenging me to continue.

"I don't know how it happened," I whispered lamely.

"Well, congrats bud," Annie laughed. "This could be your shortest relationship yet."

Groaning, I forced myself to get up from the sofa and trudged up to my room. This was going to be horrific, it was way too early to be subjected to my parents. I was going to lose her before I even got a chance to have her... in the non-biblical sense of course.

I'd have to up my game and show her I was a good guy before she ran for the hills. Starting first thing in the morning.

15 – Stripper initiation

Willow

I woke up early the next morning, surprised to find my duvet covering me on my sofa. The clock on the wall told me it was barely 7am. I stretched, nearly knocking my table lamp over and then bolted upright.

Perry had still been here when I started dozing off last night... but he was nowhere to be seen now. I looked over at the door and saw his keys were gone, along with his shoes and as much I appreciated the gentlemanly behaviour, I was acutely disappointed.

In hindsight however, it was for the best. The night had been wonderful. I had been relatively tic free and the small things that happened were easy to gloss over. I didn't even think he had noticed. It was best not to push my luck too far until I knew him a little better.

The memory of our time together stayed with me while I got myself ready for the day. His smile kept me company in the shower, his aftershave lingered on the pillows as I drank my morning brew. I was such a smitten kitten.

I was just finishing with my wayward hair, deciding it would be easier to allow the kinky curls to do their own thing, when the doorbell rang. At this time on a Saturday, it could only be the terrible twosome.

I stalked over to it, noticing my keys on the mat. Warmth spread throughout me knowing he had thought enough to lock the door behind him and put the keys back through the letterbox. He was... damn, he really was one of the good guys.

Now the impatient visitors were knocking, ruining my dreamy moment so I opened the door, already spouting obscenities about unwanted callers...

"I can go away and come back later?"

... only to find a freshly showered and changed Perry on my doorstep, with breakfast rolls in his hands.

"I'm really sorry, I thought you were Simone and Daniel."

He shrugged and walked in, stopping to drop a kiss to my head as he passed. "I wouldn't have gone away anyway. Breakfast?"

He pulled a couple of plates down and fished the packed rolls from the paper. I watched in amusement as he made himself at home in my tiny kitchen, making drinks for us both. He glanced up and offered the most genuine smile, making my heart do another of those little flutters.

Breakfast in hand, we settled into the sofa and enjoyed a comfortable silence. I was so screwed. I liked him, so much. Doubts started invading my happy thoughts, ones I didn't want to give a voice to. Like how I wouldn't fit in with his perfectionist family and how this was going to look Monday at work. Not that there was a rule against inter office relationships. Jasmine and Ben wouldn't be married if there was. I was more concerned that he would go back to being the boss, and I would just be a co-worker... almost like a dirty little secret. Which brought me straight back to Hot Steppers.

"What's brought that frown back?"

I popped the last bite of the delicious roll into

my mouth, placed the plate on the coffee table and nestled back against the cushions. "I think we need to discuss the elephant in the room."

He nods his head slowly, placed his own plate on top of mine and turned to face me full on.

"Ok, let me start." He watched me for a moment, as if he needed a few minutes to organise his thoughts. He looked so serious and I'd be lying if it didn't make me nervous. "For the last 3 years, I've been living down in Dorset. The company I used to work for have offices there as well as here in Reading. When they finally decided to relocate to Dorset fully, I told them I didn't want to make the move permanently. Reading is my home."

I wasn't sure where this was going, it certainly wasn't what I was going to talk about, but I just gave small nods to let him know I was listening and let him carry on.

"I've barely made it home in the last few years. Apart from a quick visit for the interview two months ago that is. A few of the guys had been bugging me to go out for drinks with them so on that visit, I got dragged to a club..."

Oh shit. I could see where this was going now and all I wanted to do was run for the bloody door.

"Never set foot in Hot Steppers before that night. Mainly because I knew Annie liked the place and there was no way I was watching guys get their tackle out." He smirked and grabbed a hold of my ice-cold hand. "I saw a showgirl called *B'Twitched* do the sexiest fucking dance and I was hooked. I figured I would try my luck last Saturday night and see if she was performing again. You see, I'd met this woman at work and she gave me one hell of a brush off. I was feeling a little pissed and thought a guy's night would get her off my mind. It was my lucky night. *B'Twitched* was performing again, looking ten times sexier and..."

I gulped and gripped the arm of the chair. He'd already seen me in action? But he couldn't have known it was me. Oh god, was this all an ego boost? To see if he could bag a stripper?

"Hey," he tilted my face up to meet his eyes. "I didn't know it was you to begin with. The first time I was too far back to see your face, so I didn't make the connection when I met you in the office that day. But even seeing you on stage up close, with all that war paint on your face, I didn't know straight away... until I saw Daniel Hope standing to the side of the stage looking like a cross between a proud father and a bodyguard."

Busted.

"I need you to know that, I may have thought the woman on that stage was sinful as fuck, but it was nothing compared to the way I felt when I saw you for the first time."

I sighed a little shaky breath and gripped his hand a little tighter. "I wish you'd never seen that."

"I know," he tugged my hand and pulled me over to him. Not content to have me just sit close, he pulled me onto his lap, facing him head on.

"I swear to you, I've only done that twice in my life. I know right," I laughed as his eyebrows rose in disbelief. "Both times was an

102

experiment. I'm not good with being scrutinised. You may have noticed. What better way to be under the microscope than in a strip club."

He rubbed a hand down my arm and chewed on his lip a few times. "Seems a little..."

"Farfetched?"

"I was gonna go with extreme."

I levelled my gaze at him. "There is a lot of 'extreme' behaviour in my life Perry."

The thoughtful look on his face stayed there as he took that in. "Did you... did the way I treated you have anything to do with you going back there last weekend?"

"A little..."

He groaned and dropped his head to my shoulder. "Fuck sake."

"It's not like you could have known."

"Doesn't matter."

"Yeah it does. It was my choice, my own stupid idea. It won't happen again anyway, Daniel nearly has a heart attack over the whole thing. It wouldn't have happened the first time if Ben hadn't sided with me."

"Ben Hope? Jasmine's husband... as in the Head of IT?"

I chuckled at the look of shock on his face. "Yeah, one and the same. It really helped him when he stripped there..."

"Jesus Christ. Does everyone strip there? Oh, please don't tell me Annie has..."

He was starting to look a little green. "Don't be stupid. Daniel is a regular stripper, Ben has only done it a handful of times to cover for him. I only stripped twice, and that is my lot. I promise."

"YOU DID WHAT!"

I nearly fell off Perry's lap as 5ft 10ins of very pissed off Simone stomped across my living room leaving a decidedly pale Daniel in the doorway.

I felt sorry for his balls already.

16 – Plucking Feathers

Willow

"Tell me this is a fucking joke and you didn't strip at Hot Steppers."

"Simone, it was just a couple of times..."

"Oh my fucking god!" She spun around and levelled an angry stare at her husband, one that had me wincing. "And you knew?"

"Babe..."

"You fucking knew my baby cousin was planning to take her clothes off?"

"She swears a lot huh?" Perry whispered in my ear.

This was humiliating, devastating and kinda amusing. Well, the part where Daniel leant back against the wall with his hands protectively covering his junk was amusing... the rest was not.

"It was her idea, I just made sure..."

"What? That she had the right outfit?"

"That was part of it..."

"Well aren't you a damn hero!"

"Thanks babe..."

"It wasn't a fucking compliment."

I needed to wade in here, even if it did get me flayed. Sliding off Perry's lap, I walked over and tapped on Simone's shoulder only to have her shrug me off while she continued to lay into Daniel. With a sigh, I stepped around her and stood between them. They both tried to move me out of the way, but I'd had enough by this point.

Instead they chose to shout through me, around me, over me... I could barely get a word in edgeways. Simone was livid, both at Daniel, myself and Ben to some extent. Daniel had passed the point of fear for his tackle and was now giving as good as he got in return, volleying her accusations back with some choice words of his own.

And me?

This was one giant trigger. I knew my shoulder was shrugging, my fingers were flexing... I also knew in between my attempts to interject their argument, I was swearing like a polish sailor.

"Hey!"

We all stopped and turned to face Perry. He had been sat there the whole time, listening to this embarrassing battle of wills but now he was walking over to our trio with a look of disgust on his face.

"I'm assuming you two know all about Willow's syndrome?"

Oh... crap. Simone's confused face morphed into one of absolute fury. "What the hell is *that* supposed to mean? Of course we do, she's our family."

He came to stand by my side, his arm wrapping around my shoulders before walking me back over to the sofa with him. "Then I'd love to know why the two of you would barge in here, screaming and shouting, which obviously isn't good for her. I know next to nothing about Tourette's but even I can see your behaviour is a trigger for her."

You could have heard a pin drop. My jaw had hit the floor and I didn't see it closing any time soon. Perry sunk back onto the sofa, bringing me with him. He paused for a moment, and then I was being hauled back across his lap.

Daniel and Simone were the picture of contrite across the room and as much as I wanted to take a picture to immortalise the moment, I was still struck dumb at Perry's actions. I was always furiously adamant that none of my nearest and dearest treat me any differently, but I couldn't help the smile in my soul that he had not only come to my rescue, but that he had done it without prompt.

I was a walking contradiction.

"Willow..." my sullen cousin began.

"I'm Daniel Hope," her husband interrupted, stroking her arm as he walked by. He held a hand out to shake with Perry.

"We've met."

"Really?" Daniels face scrunched up.

Perry took hold of Daniel's hand and shook it. "Annie's wedding reception. You were drunk."

Daniel clicked his fingers as if this explained everything and laughed. "Sounds exactly like me."

"I remember you now," Simone sat on the end of my sofa and fixed him with her steely gaze. "You were with that toffy nosed woman, the one that was rude to Annie."

I could feel Perry stiffen beneath me and I had to wonder who would be brave enough to insult Annie.

"Annie held her own and I put Amelia in a taxi home. No one insults my friends in my presence."

Simone continued to watch Perry as we all lapsed into an uncomfortable silence. "That won't work, you know."

I turned to catch her eye, but she was

looking at the way Perry was running his fingers over my shoulder. Although I was feeling much calmer now that the shouting was over, I was still showing the odd shrug. It would take a few minutes for me to gain a bit of control over my body again.

"Don't be a bitch…"

"No," she cut me off. "I wasn't trying to be. Promise. It's just… I've never seen you with a boyfriend before and well, it's a little strange. That's all."

It was on the tip of my tongue to set her straight. I didn't want her assuming that we were an item just yet, although I was hopeful. I didn't want Perry to feel pressured either.

"We haven't had a chance to talk about it yet, I don't know what I'm supposed to do. This just felt right."

I smiled at Perry and leant a little closer to him. "This is good."

Simone snorted. "You could try not pissing her off and sending her off to make stupid decisions with my dead husband for a start."

Perry gave her a nod and laid a hand protectively on my knee. "Oh, believe me, I won't."

The pain in the arse duo stayed much longer than I would have liked, cutting into my alone time with Perry. Now we were enjoying some pasta while I regaled him with my long winded medical history. It was the most involved and honest conversation I had ever had with a

108

potential partner.

I explained the ins and outs, how extreme conditions and emotions brought out the worst of it, how being relaxed and chilled could do the same. He was fascinated by the polish swearing and tried to get me to translate for him.

Yeah that wasn't happening. He asked what I had said to him on our first meeting and I quickly changed the subject. He'd laughed at me and swore that I would have to tell him one day.

I would take that bet.

Talking about my life was completely different from watching it in action however and as the morning wore on, he got enough action shots to make his own documentary. When the doorframe got its third kicking and telling off for the day, he watched as I succumbed to the walking boots. I could see him smiling to himself when I lectured the plant pot about leaving its mess on the floor and when I hovered close to the fridge (because my mouth wanted it to be sure it was running at the correct temperature) I realised that I hadn't needed to frighten men off with that bloody screensaver after all.

Had I just brought them back to my flat, they would have scampered without any effort from me. To the outside world, I seemed unbalanced and more than a little schizophrenic. It would be so easy for him to make a mad dash from the room and never return and if he did, I wouldn't hold it against him. But it would tell me a great deal about my judgement because for the first time, I felt like I had found someone who could handle... me.

17 – Ding, ding, we have a winner

Perry

Of all the places she could have picked to spend the afternoon, this was not what I was expecting. But it was so much better. Willow flitted from machine to machine, the sounds of people shouting in joy or frustration echoed around us and my girl looked so relaxed and happy.

In a shitty arcade.

"Why here?" I had asked her when she pulled me to a stop outside the rundown looking building.

"You'll see," she had smiled, going up on her tiptoes to kiss my lips.

The place was jam packed with all walks of life. That was the first thing that surprised me. I remembered going to places like this when I was a kid, and all I could picture were drunks that smelt of urine and kids bunking off school, just like I had been.

This was totally different though. I could still see groups of teenagers crowding around the racing games and shouting to their friends, that hadn't changed. But instead of tramps, there were families laughing around the penny slot machines and parents helping their children aim for the hoops on the basketball.

It was seriously awesome. And loud. And busy.

The guy on the slot machine next to Willow yelled as the lights began to flash and dance and pound coins began pumping out of his machine. Willow jumped up and down next to him, calling her congratulations and to the naked eye it all looked very normal.

But it wasn't... she was reacting to her surroundings and no one here was paying any attention to it. I understood at last why she loved it here so much. She could just relax, have fun, let her guard down and just... be.

I swept up behind her and snaked an arm around to hit one of the flashing buttons on her fruit machine, laughing when she shouted obscenities at me. The dials whirled around and then one by one, three cherries appeared.

"No fucking way," she laughed, backing up as her lights began to flash crazily and coins rained down into the tray to the strains of *simply the best.*

She turned in my grasp and threw her arms around my neck. "You're my new good luck charm."

"I'm the lucky one," I whispered back, like the pussy whipped pansy she had created.

She laughed and slapped at my shoulder but before I could back her up against the machine and claim those lips for the world to see, she had dropped to her knees in front of me. All kinds of thoughts paraded through my head as she smiled up at me. Fuck I was a pervert. She started pulling the coins from the tray into a plastic pot, a huge grin on her face and no matter how innocent she looked right now, all I wanted to do was hold her hair back and sink my dick in that mouth.

As if my cock had called her name, she stopped what she was doing and slowly turned her head until it was facing my pelvis. Her eyebrows rose, and she licked her lips... and suddenly it was very cramped in my pants.

"Turned on by fruit machines huh," she laughed, winking at me as she stood.

When I say stood, the cocky woman had grabbed onto my arm and pulled herself up... rubbing every inch of her sexy as fuck body along my achingly, embarrassingly ready cock as she went.

All my good intentions of going slow and steady went flying out the window. I crowded her back against the machine and pushed my pelvis into her belly. The urge to pick her up and really slam against the place I needed to be was all consuming.

"*You* turn me on, Willow," I mumbled against her lips before attacking them in a deep kiss that had my knees threatening to buckle. I needed to get her out of here and somewhere private. Didn't care where, as long as I could do something about this raging hard-on.

"Get a room," a woman laughed as she walked past us, breaking into the hazy lust I was feeling.

Willow was breathing heavily, her free hand pressed against my chest. "I think... Ummm..."

I smoothed my hands over her face, loving the dazed look I'd put on her lovely features. "What do you think Willow?"

She bit down on her full bottom lip and my cock took attention.

"I think I'd like you to take me home now," she raised her brow again and looked up into my eyes with so much trust, it nearly undid me then and there.

"Then let's go." I held my hand out for her and when she slipped hers inside, I felt a little giddy.

Shit, I really was a fucking pussy.

"Just to be clear," she called back to me as we wound around the rest of the patrons. "We're having sex today, right?"

I nearly choked on my own tongue as she winked over her shoulder and a guy next to her checked out her ass. "Fucking hell love, if he won't. I will."

"No chance," I growled, catching up to them and pulling Willow possessively into my arms.

The man laughed loudly, and I took the moment to drag my girl out of that place before I started a fight. Ok, I wouldn't have started anything, the guy was freakishly huge.

The sassy woman spun away from me and smiled. "Sorry, I couldn't resist watching you squirm."

"Just to be clear," I stalked towards her, loving how she backed away until she bumped against the wall. "You won't be needing clothes for the next few hours. Understand?"

She gulped nervously before slowly nodding her head.

I leaned in and put my lips to her ear. "Good, because I'm ready to nibble those giblets."

18 – There's a cock in my hen house

Willow

The front door banged shut behind me... the lock was thrown into place... my keys and bag were placed down by my sofa... and I was barely aware of any of this.

Because Perry Moore's lips were short circuiting my brain.

He was everywhere. His hands were in my hair, sliding down my back, grabbing at my butt. His mouth suckled at the sensitive skin at the base of my throat, only to trail a path up to the equally pleasurably spot just at the corner of my jaw.

I was in sensory overload, but I wanted more.

My hands joined the fun, running down the front of his chest and pulling at the fabric of his shirt. My fingers met with warm smooth skin, a teasing touch that had my body arching towards him, desperate to feel more.

"Fuck Willow, you taste so sweet," he groaned.

A small whimper escaped as he hauled my frame up into his arms and walked the short distance to my bedroom. We collapsed in a heap on my messy bed, laughing as we disentangled ourselves from my balled-up duvet.

Then he was back on me, my legs dropping shamelessly to the side as he settled between them.

"Is this too fast?" I moaned as his tongue traced a path down to the top of one breast. "I feel like this is fast."

"Not fucking fast enough," he answered, his

fingers pulling the vest top down until the lacy cup of my bra came into view. "Fuck it."

He sat me up, whipped my vest top over my head and shoved me back down on the bed, his fingers already working their magic on my bra. Before I could so much as moan, my boobs were meeting fresh air and the warm cavern of Perry's mouth.

"Oh my god!" I cried out, the pleasure of his hands and lips and teeth becoming all too much.

He growled against my large chest and pushed his solid cock right into the heart of me. He was trying to kill me, I was sure if it.

"Perry, I need…" I began but no words came out as he used that moment to tug the nipple on one breast with his fingers and suckle the other between his teeth.

"Shhhh," he answered. "I know exactly what you need Willow."

Doubtful, I thought to myself. *I* didn't know what I needed. I was a ball of pent up emotions, my mind on overdrive trying to process all the sensations he was bringing out in me while my body craved more. More of his touch, more of his body against my own.

The sounds of a zipper dropping hit my ears and then I was being dragged down the bed, much to Perry's amusement. My jeans slipped over the generous curves of my arse, but not without a fight. When they were that hard to get into, they didn't just magically drop off like in the movies.

Legs dangling off the edge of the bed, I sat up on my elbows ready to make a sarcastic comment, anything to take the edge off the slightly embarrassing moment, but words failed me as he stood there, silently shucking the shirt and giving me the first glimpse of what was underneath.

Can we say Adonis? White sculpted skin for miles... he was clearly defined, a much larger man than what I was used to. He was built with power in mind, the taut muscles in his strong arms belying the hours of training he must put in to look that good.

I glanced down at my own exposed torso and felt decidedly soft. Not that he had seemed to care. I wasn't one of those girls that had body hang ups, I had enough to worry about without that. I was a curvy girl for sure, but I was fit and healthy. I owned that shit.

Perry on the other hand, took fit and healthy to another level.

His jeans had dropped to the floor and if I had been impressed by his arms, that was nothing compared to the strong lines of his thighs.

"Hubba hubba," I mumbled.

He burst out laughing and walked back to me, dropping to his knees between my legs. "Does that mean you like what you see? Or are you mocking me again."

"Oh, I like," I whispered, leaning forward to get close to those delectable lips again. "I like, a lot."

He smirked and placed a hand on my chest. "Good."

His hand smoothed over my chest, down between my breasts and kept on going until he hit the top of my knickers. I watched with rapture as he dipped his hand beneath the satin and ran his fingertips across the trembling skin.

Slowly, his other hand travelled up my leg caressing my thigh on its journey. I felt the coils of anticipation unfurl deep in my belly, the look of hunger on his face as he watched his own hands was more of a turn on than anything else.

With deliberate strokes, his hands grasped the sides of my underwear and dragged the dainty material down my legs. I moaned with need, eyes focused on his, his focused on the path his fingers made.

"Hurry Perry," I murmured, aware of just how desperate I sounded and not giving a shit.

He dropped his nose to my thigh, running it along my pebbling flesh until it was within a breath of touching me where I wanted him. "I thought you said this was too fast?"

"It is!" His eyes rose to meet mine in question and I shook my head, reaching a hand out to touch his face. "But it feels too good to stop."

His answering grin was beautiful, his whole face lit up with adoration and I realised he had fallen just as fast and crazily for me as I had for him.

The sweet moment ended almost instantly however... when his face disappeared between my legs. Intense, intimate, lingering... I had a whole dictionary of words cascading through my head as he worked every single inch of my pussy until I was barely coherent.

If his fingers moved, his tongue replaced them... when his tongue travelled to a new sweet spot, the heel of his hand would work the flesh into a frenzy. I couldn't breathe, I couldn't think... I was tight, inside my tummy the anticipation had morphed into sheer lust, sheer desire and I was just along for the ride.

"Perry," I yelled out, my hands diving into his hair and grasping tight.

"Fuck," he groaned, the rumble of his voice sending more delicious waves of pleasure coursing through my body. "I need more."

He pushed with his shoulders and my body slid up the bed, his body following and his mouth never once breaking free from the job. I was slipping in and out of a pleasure induced state when he rolled the pair of us until he was on his back and I was squishing his face down into the mattress.

I sat up quickly and squinted down at his barely visible eyes. "Shit, I'm sorry," I stammered. I attempted to move but he held my thighs firmly and pushed his face further into my waiting sex.

"Don't be," he licked a path and pulled my hovering pussy down firmly. "Just ride me Willow."

I hesitated, for a second too long because he raised up, slammed his mouth back over my pounding clit and dragged us back to the bed.

"Holy shit," I yelled out, grabbing on to the top of my headboard and giving in to the rhythm. I matched his movements thrust for thrust, my leg muscles working harder than they ever had at the gym.

The tell-tale tightening in my tummy sank lower, spiralling out to my limbs. Everything was beginning to shake, and I knew, I just knew this was going to be the most intense orgasm I had ever had in my life.

118

"I'm... oh... Perry... I..."

His answering groan was all I needed, well that and the well-timed fingers he suddenly pushed inside me. I cried out as my body took on a life of its own, my thighs shuddering around his cheeks, my clit pulsing, pussy clenching and heart racing in my chest. I collapsed to the side, somehow taking Perry with me. He slowly licked my still spasming sex, while I died on the bed next to him.

"You were fucking amazing," he mumbled, dropping one last kiss directly to my clit before skimming up the bed towards my face. With a wink he said, "You were ok too."

"Ha fucking ha," I laughed quietly. I was completely wiped out; my poor body had turned to jelly.

"Thank you," he whispered.

"For what?"

"For deciding it wasn't too fast," he laughed. "But mainly for giving this arsehole a chance."

My heart flipped over, proving that it wasn't dead after all. "I should be thanking you."

"Well, I would hold that thought." He looked over to me and although he was still smiling, there was a little tightness around his eyes. "Are you relaxed?"

"I can barely move," I laughed, wondering what was on his mind.

"That's good," He jumped from the bed and slid into the bathroom. I heard the shower starting and wondered if he was gearing up for the next round. I had never had shower sex before...

"I want you to feel good," he walked back in with just a towel around his waist and a sexy smirk on those lips.

... or given head in the shower...

"Because you're so fucking special to me." He continued.

... or slow sweet kisses in the shower...

"And we're having dinner with my parents in an hour."

... I'd also never killed in the shower, but that was about to change.

19 – Meet the f***ers

Perry

I could see she was nervous.

I would give anything to reassure her, to be able to say the normal things guys said in these situations. The whole, you'll be fine, they're just regular people, they will love you just the way you are...

But I realised that lying to Willow wasn't an option. Toning a situation down to spare her feelings worked against her and I'd be damned if I sent her into an atmosphere that she wasn't prepared for.

My mother would be passively aggressive.

My dad would be there in body but not in spirit, that would be at the office still.

If my brother bothered to turn up, he would hit on her... and I would punch his fucking head in.

But worst of all, there was every chance she would have invited the *'lovely young lady'* from next door for dinner too.

I gave her everything I could on the way over, told her all the sorts of things that had happened in the past, hoping to give her a heads up. By the time we pulled into the driveway, I felt a little sick to my stomach. It wasn't the first time I'd taken someone home for dinner, but it was the first time I had given a shit how it worked out.

Willow was much more than just a new fling. I had known it the first time I saw her in that office and it had only gotten stronger. I was falling head over heels for this woman, and she was just as addicted to me.

That made me the luckiest bastard on the planet and I wasn't going to let anything get in the way of our relationship.

Even my mother, who was standing in the landing window upstairs, staring down at my car with a curious expression on her face.

"Why is she staring?" Willow peered up and quickly slunk back in the seat. "That's creepy as fuck Perry."

"Yeah," I rubbed at the back of my neck. "I got nothing. She isn't usually quite so... strange."

She sighed deeply and reached out for my hand. The simple gesture told me more than a thousand words ever could. It was on the tip of my tongue to tell her we were leaving when she leant over the console and pressed her lips against mine.

"You have no idea how much you owe me for this," she whispered.

"I know," I agreed, amazed at her strength of character as she took a deep breath and opened the door.

I met her at the front of the car, took her elbow and steered her into impending doom. I wished I could say I was exaggerating. My childhood house loomed before us, palatial in its glory. As a child, I had loved the huge house, it had been the best playground for my brother and me. Now, it just seemed over the top. Eight bedrooms for a family of four was beyond ridiculous.

"I need to know," she mumbled as we neared the porch. "Do they know anything about me?"

I knew what she was asking, and I felt like a

complete ass when I shook my head. Panic wavered on her face for a second before she locked it down.

"This should be fun," she sighed, her fingers flexing at her sides.

The front door opened before we even made it to the top of the porch steps and there stood my father looking as if he was ready for the office, just like always.

"Good evening, son," he rumbled in his rough tone. "It's about time you came to visit us. Your mother was starting to forget what you looked like."

I managed to stop myself from replying with my usual sarcasm. It usually resulted in a slanging match between my dad and I, and I didn't want Willow to be a part of that. Not that my parents were overly argumentative, I just seemed to bring out the worst in them. Just chalk it up to years of pent-up frustration.

"Good to see you too, Dad. Have you been working out?"

He appraised me for a moment and then let out a surprised laugh. "Always the wise cracker."

His gaze slid from me over to Willow and all I wanted to do was grab her up and whisk her away before she had to be subjected to these people. But deep down I knew, if I wanted her to be a part of my life, I was going to have to let this happen.

Willow surprised the crap out of me when she stepped up to my father with a hand outstretched. "It's a pleasure to meet you, sir. Perry has told me so much about you."

My dad looked from her and to me and then

took her hand gently in his. "I'm sure he has. All good I hope."

"Of course, Sir," she replied, and I had to hand it to her, I almost believed it myself.

"You'll have to forgive my son; his manners are appalling. I don't know what they teach them down there in Devon. My name is Alexander Moore, please call me Alexander."

She smiled sweetly and if I didn't know better, I would swear my dad was smitten.

"Oh, I don't know," she continued, shooting a quick look in my direction. "I find your son to have extremely good manners. You must've done something right, Alexander. I'm Willow Summers."

Then came the voice from behind my dad that I had been dreading. "So, this is the lady you've been hiding from us."

My mother stepped out onto the porch, all 5 feet 4 inches of her, and dressed in her usual finest. Her hair was swept up into one of those fancy twist things without a single strand out of place. She looked almost mechanical, and I hated it. I'd give anything to see my mum in a pair of jeans again.

"Hello Mrs Moore." I could see the unease rolling off Willow. My mother didn't extend her hand like my father had so Willow stood awkwardly for a heartbeat before clasping both hands in front of her.

I felt wholeheartedly disappointed in my mother at that moment. I knew she wouldn't go out of her way to make Willow feel welcome, but I was hoping that maybe she would prove me wrong.

"Evening Mum."

She turned her gaze on me and her eyes softened. "My son. It's been too long, young man."

She stepped forward and opened her arms for me. I stepped into her embrace, a small smile on my lips as she pressed a kiss on my cheek. Her light floral perfume, the same scent she had always worn enveloped us. I sighed and enjoyed the moment. No matter how old you grew, a good hug from your mum was always a comfort. Even a mother like mine.

"Well come along. Dinner is almost ready, and your brother is probably starving by now."

We hung back slightly, taking much longer than necessary to hang our coats up.

"Are you ok?"

She offered a little grin and leant in close. "I like your dad. Not sure about your mum, she seems kinda cold."

"I'm sorry, Willow."

She shook her head and put her arm around my neck. "Don't be. I'm a clever girl Perry, I know you aren't your parents."

"Do you also know that I'm not my brother? Because he is a real piece of work. Used to be a great guy until he decided to be a kiss arse."

She chuckled and dropped her forehead against my chest. Wrapping her up in my arms, I thought again about just running out the door and forgetting this whole night.

"Give me some credit, I can handle it."

There wasn't much I could do about it now, although it would have been nice to stagger the whole meet the family thing. At least, I thought as we began the trek towards the dining room, mother hadn't made it an excuse to invite anyone else. I had been convinced Amelia was going to show her face. That would have been an absolute nightmare. The woman was unhinged, not that my mum could see it.

"Hello Perry."

I stopped cold and wanted to die there and then on the spot. Amelia stepped out from her place in the front room, dressed to impress and every inch a carbon copy of all the women in my family's social circle. She leant against the doorframe, glass of wine in hand and a calculating look on her face.

Shit.

Her eyes slid up and down my body and I knew from the outside, she was giving a very different impression of what we were to each other. Meaning nothing, we were completely fucking nothing to each other and never had been. Not for want of her trying though.

I had done everything, and I mean everything to avoid her clutches. Since the day she moved in next door to us, she saw me as a challenge. To her, I was her meal ticket, a way to be a part of one of the most financially well-off families in Reading. She could easily go after Archie to secure a place, but in her words, she didn't feel anything for Archie.

Translated: She'll happily sit on his face and let him fuck her in the guest house, but he wasn't focused enough to be a husband. That was where I came in. Because who doesn't want their brother's sloppy seconds... shudder.

Amelia stepped up to me, completely ignoring Willow, and began to slide her hands up my arms. She reeked of Chanel, the expensive perfume so pungent I couldn't help but start coughing.

"Jesus Christ, Amelia. Did you take a bath in that perfume?"

"Reginald!" My mother scolded, and the little boy inside me gave himself a high-five. That was another record, being told off in less than 5 minutes.

"I'm surprised she's here, I thought this was a family meal," I directed towards my mum, but she had already turned on her heel and stalked away, obviously embarrassed by my lack of manners. I didn't care.

"Silly," Amelia stepped close again, clearly not getting the message that her perfume was killing me. "I'm pretty much family, we've been close for as long as I can remember."

I knew what she was trying to do, and I hated her for it. If it wasn't obvious in the way she spoke, it was implied with not so subtle looks. She was putting on a show, all for Willow's benefit and I didn't like it at all. I could see I was going to have to do a lot of damage control after this evening.

Wanting to reassure my girl and feeling protective, I pulled Willow into my side. "I think you're confusing me with Archie."

"Well, well, well. What do we have here?" *Speak of the devil,* I groaned inwardly.

My brother strolled into the hallway and made a beeline for Willow, his greedy eyes eating her up.

"How did you manage to get someone that looks like that Perry?" He sidled up to her, grabbed her hand and lifted it to his lips. "It's a pleasure to meet you, Miss Summers. I hope my brother is keeping you satisfied." He sent a wink

127

my way and it was all I could do not to rip Willow's hand back.

"I suggest you back the fuck away from my girlfriend before I break your face."

"Okay, that's enough boys," my father said, sounding as exhausted as he looked. "Archibald, if you could please show a little restraint, we don't want Willow thinking we're all animals."

He smiled at Willow and for the first time in years, I was grateful to him.

"Now," he said, pulling her away from my twat of a brother and linking her hand through his arm. "Let's go and have a nice dinner, shall we?"

I stalked past Archie and rammed my elbow into his gut. He groaned and muttered some colourful words. I hoped the bastard choked on his fucking steak.

20 - One doesn't care

Willow

If emotions had faces, they would all be sitting at this table. Alexander would be preoccupied, his wife without doubt would be contemplation. Perry's brother Archie would be lust. Maybe stupidity. Lustful stupidity. I'm certain my face would be called unease and my poor boyfriend was a dead ringer for protective.

Then there was Amelia. She, like many women before her, had two faces. The one she showed the Moore family was sweetness and light all mixed into one. The face she aimed in my direction was a whole other story.

Disgust. Anger. Resentment. Competition.

I saw it in the way she watched Perry as he placed his hand on top of mine on the dinner table. I saw it in the way her fist clenched each time Perry smiled in my direction and when he leant towards me to whisper in my ear, she practically turned green with envy.

Now, I wasn't the type to gloat over getting the man, but she was making it really hard to be gracious about it. Perry had assured me that there had never been anything between the two of them and although I believed him, it's quite clear she desperately wanted there to be.

From the outside looking in she was everything that fit in with this family. She obviously came from money, knew what knives and forks to use and when to use them, and had an air about her that screamed grace and breeding. From the tips of her perfectly manicured nails to her elegantly styled auburn hair, she was flawless.

I, on the other hand, was entirely too working-class, too dark skinned, and as soon as my body tripped me up, I would be considered too defective to ever be a member of this world. The sensible thing to do would be to end it now before I really got hurt. But I wasn't sensible, and Perry was worth the risk.

It was about halfway through the second course when my nerves finally began to settle. I was still anxious, and I was still holding myself rigid but there was something about having Perry next to me that made me feel safe. No more than a few seconds went by without Perry touching me in some way, a foot slipping over to touch mine or a hand on my leg. It made me forget I was under a microscope.

My tics were behaving somewhat. Sure, my fingers rebelled and danced a tune, as did my wayward shoulder, but I was a pro at hiding the signs when I was under pressure. I did it every day at the office and tonight was no different.

Conversation had been flowing around what was happening with Perry's older brother (apparently, he was an executive car salesman, but the eye roll from Perry had me wondering just how "executive" he really was) and then it was focused on Perry's new position with the Gold Dime Group. I was happy to keep quiet and listen, anything that kept the focus off me.

"I understand you work with our son, Willow," Belinda Moore, Perry's mum, suddenly piped up. It was the first thing she had said directly to me the whole evening. She was an intimidating little woman. She hadn't outright looked down her nose at me, but she hadn't acknowledged me either and I wasn't sure which was worse. Disdain would be nasty but at least I would know where I stood.

"Yes," I replied. "I've worked for the company for 18 months now."

She seemed surprised, which didn't surprise me in the least. "What exactly is it you do?"

"I'm part of the marketing crew. I essentially design mock-ups for the latest brands that we are going to be representing, or rebranding those that are on our records already."

"And she's damn good at it too," Perry interjected with pride.

Belinda glanced his way and offered a genuine smile towards her son before focusing back on me. "What of your family? Are you originally from Reading?"

This was the part I had been dreading. His family was no stranger to Reading, and I felt positive they would know the good areas from the bad. Grindley was most definitely in the bad part. I was prepared for the look on her face when I told her where I had come from, but it was nothing compared to the look of disgust on Amelia's face.

"I'm a bit confused." Amelia made a show of putting her finger to her chin, as if deep in thought. "I thought it was all black people that came from there."

"Amelia!" Perry chided.

"No, it's okay." I placed a hand on his leg and give it a squeeze. He might not like it, but I was used to defending myself, had been doing it for years. Although admittedly, it wasn't usually over race. "You're quite right Amelia, there's many ethnic families in Grindley. It's beautifully

131

diverse and as you can see, I fit right in with all colour codes."

Everybody was so focused on me, they didn't see the smirk she passed in my direction. Her eyebrows raised in challenge, for what I had no clue. There were plenty of mixed race and different ethnic families right here in The Warren, so her angle was throwing me. It didn't pay to be racist in their particular social circle. What was she playing at?

"I remember reading somewhere," she continued. "That decent job prospects over in that area of Reading are few and far between. You're very lucky to have found such an advantageous position within Perry's company."

I wasn't touching that statement with a barge pole. I didn't consider luck to have anything to do with it. I worked hard, built up my portfolio and applied for the job just like everyone else. Instead of going to battle however, I smiled and went back to cutting up the delicious steak on my plate. Say what you will about these people, but the food was to die for.

"Do you still live there now?" Archie asked.

I swallowed quickly and took a sip of wine to wash it down. Damn, how was a woman supposed to get any food down? "No, I have an apartment just inside the city."

"Ahh so you must go out a lot? Where do you tend to party?"

I shrugged and gave my head a little shake. "I don't. I'm not much of a drinker and I'm not fond of large crowds or packed clubs. I prefer to be at home or spend time with friends."

"I don't blame you Willow," Alexander remarked. "Sensible girl."

Perry's dad raised a glass in my direction and I couldn't help but smile towards him. I liked him. Not once had he made me feel out of place this evening. I couldn't understand what the divide between he and Perry was about.

"I'm sure I've seen you somewhere before," Archie mused, running his eyes over my face and down my body. It was more inquisitive than anything, but I felt awkward under his attention. His mother watched on, an unimpressed frown on her face as he continued to stare in my direction.

Perry stiffened beside me. "You haven't," he stated abruptly, and the moment was over. I would have to remember to ask Perry what that was about later. I wasn't sure that I liked Archie. I knew his type – flirty and harmless, but not someone I wanted to spend time with.

"I'm quite fascinated by the work you and my son do Willow," Belinda began, blessedly changing the subject. "Tell me, how does one..."

"Mississippi," I blurted.

Fuck my life.

The whole room stopped, all eyes on me... and I wanted to shrink in my seat. "So sorry, I have a frog in my throat."

All the crappy acting skills I possessed went into coughing into my hand and making a production of swallowing some water. Perry ran his hand up and down my back, trying to soothe me. Dammit, I had been doing so well!

"It's quite alright," she started again, although she seemed far from convinced with my answer. "As I was saying, I wonder how one..."

"Mississippi."

133

Again, with the coughing. This time it had been whispered but still... the stifled laughter from Amelia said it all.

Perry did his best to cover for me, but I could tell from the looks on their faces that it didn't matter what was said from here on out. They knew something wasn't right with me. And that made me unacceptable.

And every person in this room was looking at me as if I was crazy.

I excused myself to the toilets and quickly scurried from the room, hoping Perry would just explain for me and then we could forget about this whole business. I didn't like feeling so exposed and something about his family was bringing that feeling in spades.

I splashed a little water on my face and sighed. *Mississippi.* I had no idea where it came from or why it only popped out when someone said *one...* like most elements of Tourette's, it was completely random. I didn't usually have to worry about it, I mean, who the hell still uses the word *one* like that?

Oh yeah, I thought sarcastically, posh people. Silly me.

Once I felt more myself, I opened the bathroom door and stepped out into the hallway, only to find myself face to face with the queen of bitch, Amelia.

"So, Perry tells us you're retarded."

Small minded, uneducated, ridiculously snooty rich bitch!

That's exactly what I would have called her if we had been anywhere but his parent's house. Instead I chose to walk past her and ignore her petty, and might I add rude remark.

"This farce you call a relationship won't last five minutes, Willow," she called after me.

I stopped myself, turned to face her, head held high. "Oh really?"

"Of course, it won't," she came closer until I could breathe nothing but the stench of her over applied perfume. "Clearly, you're a charity case, Perry doing his bit for society. He needs a woman who can stand by him in his world. Someone who knows how to act in public."

She leant in closer still and I had to fight the urge to lean away from her nastiness. "He needs a woman that will give him healthy babies too. The only thing you'll give him is a bunch of inbred children that can't even tie their own shoes."

"I suggest you get the fuck away from my girlfriend before I put you on your arse."

Amelia jumped away from me, her hand pressed to her chest in shock. "Perry! I was just helping Willow find her way back to the dining room."

"Why? Because she's a *retard*?" he spat venomously.

He closed the gap between us all and slipped his arm around my waist. "Stay the hell away from Willow, and stay the hell away from me too. Do you understand me?"

She looked like she was going to throw up as she frantically shook her head and ran towards the front door. I could hear Perry's mother calling her name, but I just didn't care.

"We're going," Perry stated.

I gave a small nod and let him lead me through the house.

"Where are you going?" his mother's shrill

voice carried through the hall behind us.

Perry stopped to help me with my coat and shot a look of disgust in his parent's direction. "She's a bitch. I just caught her verbally assaulting Willow. I'll say this once and once only *mother*, if you want to see me, cut all ties with that woman."

She gasped as he ushered me out the door. If I never stepped foot in that house again, it would be too soon.

21 – I don't wanna talk

Willow

"What's going on with you?"

I tipped far more sugar than was necessary into my cup and kept stirring. Coffee Nirvana was packed out this morning as was the norm for Mondays. Owen had kept up a steady stream of conversation as we waited to fill our usual orders but if I was being honest, I hadn't heard a word he'd said.

"What do you mean?"

He chuckled and took the fifth packet of sugar from my hand. "This? You're already well on your way to a diabetic coma."

My eyes rolled but I didn't argue the point. "Nothing really, just a bit nervous about how today is going to go."

His face screwed up adorably. "Meaning what? Is there a meeting I don't know about?"

"No," I sighed, reaching for another packet to drop into my cup.

How could I explain this to him without getting a lecture? And he would lecture me. Or take the piss out of me and right now I didn't know which would be worse. I mean, last week we had been laughing about the new boss and how I couldn't stand him... this week? I was desperate to see him and didn't know what his reaction in the office was going to be.

So much had happened between Perry and I in such a short amount of time, I was still reeling from it. Friday night had been wonderful... Saturday had been more than I could ever hope for in a first date. Then

Saturday night had occurred, and it had been, well, brutal.

The drive back to my apartment had been silent and while I knew I needed to talk to him about what had happened at his parents, I wasn't ready. Not while it had been so fresh in my head. The hurt that woman had caused still sat in my chest. Yesterday had been spent at my cousins, my little surrogate nieces had a field day using me as their own personal Barbie doll and I had enjoyed a break from all the thoughts swirling around in my mind.

Simone, bless her, had watched warily but didn't press me for information. It must have been killing her, but she kept quiet. Daniel however, had used every possible opportunity to pry. I had drawn the line when he followed me into the bathroom.

Freak.

Perry hadn't been silent either. 11 text messages. 4 voice messages. All of them telling me that he was ready to talk whenever I was. That he missed me. That his day was boring without me.

And with each one, my heart had melted a little more. As much as I had wanted to ring him, or invite him over, I knew I needed a little time to get my head straight. I didn't blame him for the actions of his family, but I also knew the problem wasn't going to go away. His mother had looked distraught when we walked out the door, the first real bit of emotion I had seen from her all evening and I couldn't help but feel like it was all my fault.

Not what the stuck-up bitch Amelia had said to me, I held her completely accountable for that. But the fact that there was an issue in the first place... that was all down to me. Indirectly at least.

Just thinking about that nasty piece of work had my blood boiling. She was all that was wrong with the world as far as I was concerned. How someone could be so uninformed, so judgemental of another human being just blew my mind.

"Is this something to do with our new leader and the googly eyes he makes at you when he thinks no one is looking?"

Stunned, I swivelled to face my friend. "Peacocks need love too."

Owen raised his eyebrows. "Well shit! It must be serious if he's advanced from chickens!"

"Shut up," I grumbled, giving his shoulder a shove. "You know it's random."

"Nope," he continued, popping the p. "I've told you, I don't believe that."

I laughed and shook my head. Owen had done more research on my condition than any other person in my life. He was a regular helper at the drop-in centre I volunteered at, helping with under 18's that were learning to deal with their own situations. He was constantly getting into debates with some of the more in the know helpers at the centre due to his belief that Tourette's outbursts were linked to the subconscious and that the words chosen were more poignant than we gave them credit for. While that was sometimes the case, I was also convinced that my poultry habit was in no way one of them.

"Dupek," I muttered.

"Hey! I'm not a dick," he leant in close. "And

that wasn't a tic so don't even try it."

"I wasn't going to," I laughed, pushing away from the counter and heading for the door.

The walk to the office was short and it was one of those mornings when I wished it was longer. My sigh caught his attention and he stopped on the pavement, moved us out of the way and fixed me with his earnest gaze. "Talk to me Will."

"Fine," I relented. "We had dinner Friday night. We spent Saturday at the arcade. Then we had the dinner from hell with his stuck-up parents, perverted brother and his obsessed bitch of a friend."

He blinked, his mouth flapping open. "How the hell did all that happen?"

"I really don't know."

We began walking again and I could see the cogs turning in Owen's head. "So, you like him?"

My shoulders shrugged but without thought I whispered, "Yes."

"And he likes you?"

"This is all feeling very high school right now."

"I know right," he squealed. "Did he like, hold your hand?"

"Oh my god," I laughed, clutching onto my sides. "You are such a dick!"

"Don't you mean Dupek," he waggled his eyebrows.

I grabbed his arm and started dragging him towards our building, a huge smile on my face and a lighter feel in my chest.

"Seriously though," he muttered as we joined the queue for the elevator. "Don't overthink this.

Just see where it takes you."

Yeah sure, I thought, easy as that.

"Does anyone have anything to add?"

One or two arms raised in the air, colleagues wanting to show off a little to our new boss. Everything had already been covered, in amazing detail I might add. Perry had surprised us all by calling a department meeting first thing, directing us all into the conference room where hot drinks and breakfast pastries were waiting.

There he had proceeded to go through all our projects, see where we were at and let us know what was new for our team. The meeting had been upbeat and informative, and I was shocked to discover that he brought a lot of useful insight to the table.

Not that I had thought for one minute that he was stupid or uninterested... I guess I had been too caught up in the man himself to give his position much thought.

One by one the room emptied, and it suddenly became clear that if I didn't haul ass, I was going to be left alone in this room with him. The question was whether I wanted that to happen or not.

"Miss Summers, a word please," Perry called just as I was about to escape.

I saw Owen glance back, his eyes passing from Perry to myself. I gave him a small smile, not wanting him to worry... and he lifted his fingers, discreetly giving the universal symbol

141

for banging. I was gonna kill him.

"I want you to tie up any loose ends you have today, tomorrow at the latest. We've been given the go ahead to get the Gold Tech project on the road and I need to have a team assigned asap. Do you think you can give me your recommendations by the end of the day?"

What was this now? My eyes narrowed as I dropped back down into one of the chairs, deliberately picking one that was at a safe distance from Perry. "I thought I was going to have to reapply?"

He was shaking his head before my sentence had even ended. "I have no grounds to do that. Your pitch was approved by Jasmine herself, she wants you to head the account and after examining some of your other work, I have to agree you're the best one for the job."

I toyed with the edge of my blouse and tried not to look at him. "This isn't..."

"Isn't what?"

"Pity?"

He sucked in a sharp breath and stood from his chair. He was walking towards me and I just wanted him to stop. A day apart had done little to stop the feelings that were building for him, but this wasn't the time. I had to know I was here because I deserved to be.

The chair next to me pulled out and he swivelled it around to face me before he spoke. From the outside, we looked like we were having a normal conversation... inside this room though, the air was thick with unspoken words.

"In this building, when we're working, I promise you it's all business." He leant forward and rested his elbows on his knees. "We have a job to do and I will treat you the same as everyone else in this department."

I blew out a relieved breath and gave a small nod. "So, my being on the Gold Tech account?"

"Is because you earned the spot fair and square."

I smoothed my sweaty hands down over my skirt and stood up. "Thank you, Mr Moore."

I barely made it an inch when his hand caught onto my thigh. "But Willow?"

I glanced down to where his hand met with my leg, not quite high enough to be intimate but by no means innocent.

"Business hours are 9 to 5. The rest of the time, you're mine."

"Perry…"

"We'll talk later, and we *will* talk."

My fingers tapped against my other leg and he quickly dropped his hand away.

"What if I'm not ready to talk Perry?"

He smiled and stood from his seat. "Then you can listen."

22 – Damage control

Perry

"How was your day honey."

I laughed as Annie helped me remove my coat and flitted around like a fifties housewife.

"Gee darling," I drawled. "What a wonderful welcome!"

She cackled and shot me the bird, a sure sign that my friend hadn't been body snatched. The smell of Italian cooking wafted through the house and I had to stifle a groan. It smelt awesome, but if Annie had cooked it...

"Nearly ready mate, take a seat," Jason called out as I walked into the kitchen diner. He laughed at the relieved look on my face. "I cooked, no worries."

"Hey!" Annie yelled.

"Look, we all know your skills in the kitchen have nothing to do with why I married you. Own that shit babe."

She shot him a saucy wink and I tried not to gag. The downside to living with a couple like Jason and Annie was that they had no boundaries. I'd only been here shy of a month and I had lost count of how many times I had walked in on them mid thrust. It was disturbing... and the reason why I absolutely refused to use the butter.

I still shuddered at the thought. Some things couldn't be unseen.

"How did it go with Willow today," Annie asked as she laid the table.

I groaned and dropped down into one of the chairs. Jamie gave me a toothy grin from his highchair. "It was ok I guess. She isn't ready to talk yet."

"Well, work isn't the time anyway."

"I know," I sulked.

She rubbed her hand over my dishevelled hair and took the seat next to me. "Are you really surprised it was a disaster? I mean, your family is a pissing nightmare."

My hands rubbed over my face as I thought about it. "If it had been down to something my parents or the twat had said, it would be easier to deal with. But it was Amelia that fucked it all up. I can't believe she's still hanging around, trying to get her way. How the fuck do you get away from someone like that?"

"I know some people," Jason said as he placed the steaming lasagne down in the centre of the table.

"I don't think an assassin is the answer, but thanks anyway."

"You sure?" Jason dished up a healthy portion and started chomping. "Not even just to rough her up a little?"

Tempting.

"I still don't get why she doesn't just marry Archie," Annie mused. "At least she'd be in the club. Surely she knows you and she are never going to happen."

Wasn't that just the million-dollar question. She and Archie had been bumping uglies for years. She didn't know I knew that, but Archie had a habit of recording their sessions and sending them to me. I think he thought it was a way to have one up on me. But all it really did was make me chuckle. I'd only ever seen enough of the home videos to know it was legitimate before wanting to throw up.

My brother had the ugliest arse on the planet.

"I don't know. This whole mess is making my head hurt."

"You need a game plan…"

"Fuck yes!" Annie yelled, interrupting her husband. "I'm a pro at game plans."

"Aww really? Not this shit, it's Ben and Jasmine all over again!"

"Excuse me?" Annie glared at him. "It worked out perfectly last time."

"It nearly didn't Annie."

"Whatever," she turned her hand over to examine her nails. "They're happily married now aren't they?"

The crazy couple started to bicker, and I lost myself in my thoughts. Amelia was going to be a problem, I knew it, Willow knew it. What I didn't know was just how much of a problem she was going to be.

The only thing I was sure of, Willow was worth fighting for… and I never backed down from a challenge.

"I'm telling you, the waitress wants me."

"You're delusional."

"Are you kidding me? Who wouldn't want a piece of this?"

I watched in amusement as Daniel Hope stood from his chair and strutted, yes, I said strutted, over to the bar and made a play for the lady that had brought our drinks to the table.

The very uninterested lady that was at least twice my age.

"Is he always so..."

"Yes," Ben Hope sighed, lifting his pint to his lips and shaking his head at his brother. "We think he needs psychiatric help."

"He'll go home tonight, tell Simone about the hot waitress that came onto him and that he had to beat her off while professing to the entire pub that he's a one-woman man."

I gaped at Jason. "And what does that achieve?"

"Fucking hot sex my friend!" Daniel dropped back into the chair next to me and slapped my back. "Off the fucking charts, animalistic fucking of epic proportions."

"I think I just threw up in my mouth," Ben choked.

I laughed and settled back in my chair, letting the stress float away. It had been a shit week. Now that the team was assembled to work on the new account, it had been full steam ahead getting the project underway. That meant I had been within touching distance of Willow every damn day.

Do you know how hard it is to be so close to what you want and not be able to touch? I promised her it would be all about work when we were in the office, but I didn't expect her to stick to it so rigidly. Not a single stolen kiss, lingering touch of hands or even a sexy look to tide me over. To top it off, she wasn't ready to talk outside of work either.

It was killing me.

I knew now that it wasn't only the memory of that messed up dinner at my parents that was worrying her, it was the office gossip too. Everyone knew there was something going on between us thanks to the nosy fucker that had seen us in the park that day.

There were whispers when I walked out of the break room, knowing looks whenever I called her into the office... it was pissing me off to no end and I hated to think what it was doing to my girl.

Not that she would tell me.

I had asked her if I could come over every day and each time she looked like she wanted to say yes but stopped herself. What the hell was going on in that brain of hers.

"So, you and Willow huh?"

Ben leaned both elbows on the table and sent a smile my way. This was the first time I had been out with him socially and I had to admit, he was a nice guy. Quiet, polite... the opposite of his loudmouth brother.

"I'm hoping so. I seem to be striking out right now though."

"I remember the feeling well," he chuckled. "It wasn't an easy road for me and Jasmine."

I regarded him for a moment. "Because of the stripping?"

He looked surprised and shot a narrowed glance at his brother.

"Oh shit no, I didn't get that from Daniel," I grimaced, realising I had most likely just dropped Willow in the shit.

"Oh. From your girl then."

"Yeah, she was explaining how things went down the first time she stripped..."

"What the hell do you mean *'the first time'*? She's only done it once!"

148

Fucking hell, I thought, rubbing my hands down my face and wondering how many times I was going to put my foot in my mouth tonight.

"It's my fault."

His glare, which had been aimed at his brother (who was completely oblivious by the way) turned full force on me and let me tell you, for a shy IT nerd... the boy had glare.

And so, I sat there, in the middle of a rowdy pub on a Friday night and bore my soul like a pansy ass fucking girl. To his credit, Ben sat there and listened to the whole story intently and didn't once try to punch my face in.

"That's quite a tale. I have to say, I'm impressed you survived the wrath of Simone."

"I think that was more luck than anything else."

He chuckled and grabbed his pint glass. "You know what I think?"

I shook my head sullenly and waited.

"I think you're reading way too deeply into this. Willow isn't the type to place blame onto the wrong people. She won't hold your family's attitude, the gossip at work or the crazy ex against you. Sorry, bad choice of words," he amended when I was about to protest that Amelia was crazy but in no way my ex. "I think her needing time has more to do with her own issues."

"What do you mean?"

"I mean," he said, while taking my pint away from me and sliding my car keys over. "Why don't you go and see for yourself."

23 – The tic that won't quit

Willow

Things weren't going well.

That was the understatement of the century. Things were very, very fucking bad. I was living in a state of perpetual anxiety and I couldn't see a way out of it. You would think by now I was used to people looking at me, whispering about me... but truthfully, it hadn't been an issue at work. Nobody really knew about my condition because I had it in hand while I was there. Ergo, no fishbowl feeling.

But now? I was at the centre of the best kind of gossip for an office – an illicit affair.

Yep you heard it. Apparently, Perry and I were having a torrid affair and with him being the new guy and my boss, this was the jackpot for the gossip hounds. They whispered when I walked by, they stared at me when I talked to Perry, even when it was in front of other colleagues and unlikely to be me asking for a quickie.

I couldn't even go to the bathroom anymore. I had been in one of the stalls the other day when a couple of the cronies walked in and started talking about me and Perry in the most graphic terms and I was stuck there, not wanting to leave the stall and make my presence known.

Then when I did finally get to leave, it sparked more rumours.

Do you think he made her cry? Maybe she was taking a pregnancy test. Oh my god, maybe it's morning sickness! Poor girl...

Kill. Me. Now.

Between this new development, the long hours I had been putting in on the new account and the focused concentration it had taken not to show any emotion towards Perry, I was a hot mess.

And that meant, when I finally got home... I was an even hotter mess.

The tics were harsh. What was usually roughly an hour of release when I got home had turned into hours of shoulder jerking, doorframe kicking and polish abuse. My head was pounding to the point where I wanted to scream and I'm pretty sure I had just broken my big toe.

I was miserable, tired and above all, in pain.

And I missed Perry. He had asked constantly if he could see me and I so badly wanted to say yes... but I couldn't let him see me like this. I didn't want anyone to see how dreadful things had gotten this week. Simone was on the verge of dragging me to live with them, like that wouldn't send my anxiety spiralling further out of control.

I was rethinking everything about my life. Maybe I couldn't hack more responsibility at work. Maybe I should step down. Maybe I should just transfer to a different department... maybe I should answer the door and tell whoever it is that I don't speak English, so they'll leave me the hell alone!

I trudged over and wrenched the door open without even bothering to look through the peephole and my practised brush off died on my tongue when I came face-to-face with the object of my desire.

"Hey."

One word. One word was all it took. I felt my lip wobble and was horrified to feel a single tear slip from the corner of my eye. Perry glanced to my hands as they flexed repeatedly at my side, up to my shoulder as I shrugged desperately and finally, he stopped on my face.

His eyes softened with concern and before I could tell him this wasn't a good time, I was swept up into his arms.

Safe.

My body shuddered, my face burrowed into his broad chest and I wept. I was dimly aware that he had shut the door behind us and was moving us back into the room. He dropped onto my couch and pulled me down onto his lap, his arms never leaving my body.

He didn't say a word, just stroked his hand over my arms, my back. He kissed my forehead and smoothed the hair away from my face... he comforted me without uttering a sound.

I think that was the moment I fell in love with Perry Moore.

✓✓✓

"Is this why you've been avoiding me?"

I took another bite of the pizza he had ordered us and gave a small nod. He had been here for over an hour now and I was finally starting to gain back some of my composure. I had to hand it to the man, he had the patience of a saint. Who knew?

"It hasn't been a good week," I offered meekly.

He watched me for a moment. "Can I ask

what's triggering the tics?"

I sighed and sank back into the cushions. "Do you want the short version?"

He smiled and pulled my legs up onto his lap. "I want the Willow version."

I mulled it over in my mind and decided if he cared enough to be here, he deserved to know what he was getting himself into. Hell, he'd seen half the show tonight anyway. "It's just been such a shit week. When I get home from work I usually take a while to decompress but for the last few days, it's been worse."

"Because of the extra work?"

"Probably a little," I confessed. "But I think it also has a lot to do with being in the spotlight all bloody day long."

"You noticed that too huh?" he chuckled.

My fingers knotted in the hem of my raggedy hoodie. He probably thought I was ridiculous, letting the office gossip get to me.

"That's an easy fix. They won't have anything to whisper about when we come out. I'll address the team first thing Monday."

"What?"

"Look for one..."

"Mississippi."

He stopped, smiled and rubbed my leg. "I kinda love that."

"Ugh."

"What?" he laughed. "It's cute."

I snatched my leg away and hugged it to my chest. "You did not just call one of my tics cute."

"I really did."

"It's not funny Reginald."

His laughing stopped and slowly he turned to

153

face me, his eyes narrowed. "Did you just say what I think you said?"

"I really did."

His head shook from side to side in utter disbelief... and then he pounced. I squealed and tried to twist away from him, but he was too quick and way too strong. He had me pinned underneath him, his legs caging my own, his hand holding my arms above my head and a devilish look on his handsome face. I knew it was coming, anyone in this position knows when they're about to get tickled and I couldn't let that happen, so I did the only thing I could think of.

"Kiss me."

He didn't pause, didn't falter. He just took my lips with abandon, a groan sounding from deep in his throat as he sank into the kiss. He let go of my wrists, his body stretched out over mine, covering me from head to toe. I was encompassed, protected. Loved.

My fingers sought out the soft locks of his hair and tangled in them as my lips opened to his demanding kiss. It was all consuming, passionate and everything a girl dreams of. A soft sigh escaped me when he pulled back and stroked a finger down the side of my face.

"We'll tell them all on Monday," he whispered.

I shook my head gently. "It's too soon."

He smiled and pressed his lips lightly against mine. "Says who? Are you here with me Willow?"

"Obviously," I sassed, rolling my hips beneath him.

His eyebrow shot up and a fire lit in those deep sexy eyes of his. "I'm not going anywhere. I

154

want to see where things go with us, but you have to let me in. Don't hide from me."

My teeth pulled at my bottom lip. "I've never done this before. The whole including someone in my... routine, I mean. It's not pretty Perry."

"Well then," he smiled and pushed the hair back from my face. "Just as well I'm pretty enough for the both of us."

24 – Making Memories

Perry

I never thought I'd be the type of person to watch someone sleeping. Then again, I never had a Willow before.

The sun was just starting to rise, and while it was almost unheard of for me to be awake at 6am on a Saturday morning, here I was lying beside the most beautiful and intriguing woman in the world... watching her rest.

And apparently, I was pussy whipped.

Her thick, shiny hair spread about the pillow, the curls that she often tamed back in full force. The blanket flowed about her smooth caramel skin. Skin that I knew smelt of cinnamon. Willows lips were parted slightly as she sighed in her sleep and I wondered if she was dreaming of me.

Last night had been eye opening. It hadn't occurred to me how Willow would be coping with the events of the past week and I felt like a total arsehole for not having the sense to ask her outright. I knew she didn't hold it against me but fuck, I was pissed at myself.

She had told me what feelings made her condition worse. I knew that stress and anxiety were triggers for her, and yet it didn't register in my thick head that she would be suffering.

It wasn't going to happen again. I would show her that I could be someone she turns to when she needs help, comfort... anything she needs.

"Penny for your thoughts?"

Those deep amber eyes were blinking open sleepily and damn if she didn't look like all my school boy fantasies come to life. I reached over and ran the tips of my fingers along the bare skin of her arm.

"Just wondering when you were going to wake up."

She smiled, and her eyes dropped closed again. "It's too early."

"You really gonna leave me hanging?"

"Depends," she mumbled around a yawn. "What did you have in mind?"

She rolled to her back and stretched her arms up above her head, the movement causing the cover to slip and reveal the thin camisole she had worn to bed.

I gulped.

Her much more than a handful breasts strained against the material, the outline of her nipples poking up and teasing the shit out of me. It was all I could do not to grab a hold of the bloody thing and rip it from her body.

"I have a few ideas..." I whispered, losing the battle with my subconscious and leaning my head towards the generous curves.

My lips took over, ghosting over the fabric and gently kissing the tips. She gasped quietly, her body stilling and as much as I knew I should probably stop to see if this was ok, I didn't want to break the spell. Instead I reached for her hand and laced our fingers together, relieved when she gripped tightly onto me. Her other hand worked its way into my hair, something I had noticed she was fond of doing and that was all the green light I needed.

I kissed my way up her body, dragging the flimsy cotton as I went. Her body bowed beneath me, easing my way and before long I found myself chest-to-chest, skin on skin with this beautiful woman. It wasn't like me to take my time, to want to savour every moment. I'm not sure when exactly it happened but everything in my soul convinced me to make memories with Willow, not meaningless frantic groping.

I could feel it on a genetic level... this was exactly where I was supposed to be, and I wasn't going to do anything to fuck it up.

She watched my face intently as I pushed down the bottoms of her pyjamas, her eyes hooded and heavy. I loved that it was me making her feel this way. My hand smoothed over her thigh, kneading the flesh as I got nearer to the centre of her. She smiled sweetly and raised her head so she could reach my lips.

I groaned against her mouth, the sound turning into a growl as she worked a hand into my boxers and grabbed a handful of my arse. She grinned into our kiss and broke away.

"Are you gonna get to the point Perry? It's rude to make a lady wait."

"Are you sure it's not too soon?" I threw her favourite line back at her and she giggled, pretending to think on it for a moment.

"If I thought it was too soon..." She reached into the drawers by her bed and produced a huge box of condoms. "I wouldn't have bought these yesterday."

Stunned, I gaped at the 20 plus box. "You weren't even talking to me yesterday."

"Don't judge me," she laughed.

"I feel so violated!"

"Aww," she whispered. Her fingers prised at the lid and pulled one of the packets out.

158

"Maybe this will help."

One of the sexiest images in the world is a woman ripping a condom wrapper open with her teeth... just saying.

Scrap that, I thought as Willow rolled me onto my back and then made a show of looking after my saluting dick – THAT was the sexiest image in the fucking world. This *making memories* shit was awesome.

She smiled and laid back down, a what are you waiting for look on her face and I wasn't going to wait to be asked twice. Our lips met once again but this time there was a sense of urgency in the kiss. Our bodies started to move together, slowly at first and then when we were both getting to the point of no return I finally, finally, sank myself deep inside.

Our eyes locked and if I didn't know she was the one for me before, it all became clear right then. No one had ever felt this right, this perfect. I pulled out, hating to be away from her even for that long, and thrust back into her on a groan.

"Oh my god," she breathed, her hands gripping onto my back and scoring the flesh.

"Fuck, Willow."

My hips got on board and picked up the pace, hating to pull back but fucking loving driving back home. Each thrust seemed deeper than the last and I had the fleeting thought that I wasn't going to be able to hold out for long. Not with a pussy this tight and perfect gripping my cock for all it was worth.

"I need you to... fuck!" I gasped, her walls clenching me tightly and cutting off any chance of talking. Her head threw back on the pillow as she shook beneath me, her body locking up tight and then shattering around my thrusting cock.

She cried out, nails digging into my skin and thank fuck she went when she did because that was all it took for my restraint to break and my cock to jerk inside her. I collapsed onto her chest, face buried in those fantastic tits.

"Ok, maybe it wasn't too early," she whispered.

I had to agree. Best Saturday morning ever.

25 – Can't take me anywhere

Willow

"No."

"What do you mean no?"

"I mean no."

"That's not an answer."

"Well it's the only one you're going to get."

"You can't tell me what to do!"

"And yet I just did."

"Ugh!" I stomped my foot (yes, I said stomped like a sulky teenager) and turned away from the glaring man in front of me. Of course, that meant I was instead looking at the chuckling faces of the people that were meant to be my friends.

I had wanted to do something normal with Perry, but the thought of going out on a date had filled me with dread. Not because I didn't want to go out with him, far from it. I just didn't think it was such a clever idea when I had already had the tic week from hell.

So instead, we were camped out at Annie and Jason's house. Ben and Jasmine were here too... and unfortunately that meant Simone and Daniel had dropped in. Now I loved my cousin, and I loved her husband too. But not when it came to ordering takeout.

"Is no one else going to wade in here?"

Ben, ever the gentleman, jumped to my rescue. "You picked last time Dan, it's Willow's choice."

"Not a fucking chance, she'll pick Chinese. Fuck that shit."

"Oh my god! I'm not sitting here while the

twuntwaffle over there gets all precious," Annie yelled. "Let's just go to *King's*? It has everything there, buffet style all you can eat."

"But..."

Annie cut off whatever Daniel was going to say with a glare that would make anyone flinch. "Heavily. Fucking. Pregnant. Do. Not. Piss. Me. Off!"

He got to his feet and grumbled all the way to the door about how the world would be a lot simpler if he was king. Now that was a disturbing thought. Images of mandatory naked Wednesdays flitted through my mind. I shuddered.

The grumbling continued all the way to the restaurant. We had opted to go out in two cars and although we'd all made a dive for Jasmine's, somehow Perry and I had drawn the short straw and ended up in Daniel's. Even the soothing circles Perry was tracing on my palm didn't drown out the bellyaching he was doing.

In truth though, I was glad for the distraction. I had only been to King's once and that had been a nightmare. It was always packed to the gills and the whole walking around and picking your food, although a stellar idea for most, caused deep anxiety for me.

I had spent the entire time holding myself in check, so much that I had barely eaten a thing and had to get Simone to stop at a McDonalds drive thru on the way home. Complete and utter failure. However, I knew that if I was going to give the whole dating thing my all, I was going to have to try to be more social. It seemed like, surrounded by friends was the best time to start.

As I suspected, the place was hopping. I had to hand it to them, the food looked amazing and the various fragrances came together to form an intoxicating aroma. Perry had his arm about my waist as we walked to our table. It was a small gesture but one that made me feel so at ease.

Which was why, when I would have normally been on my guard, I didn't realise I was finger flexing... at least I didn't until my hand brushed against something it shouldn't have.

"Hey!"

Cursing inwardly, I turned to apologise to the older gentleman, only to have my mouth falter along with my traitorous fingers. "You have to get a good grip when you choke the chicken."

The woman, who I assume was his daughter, burst out laughing and slapped a hand over her mouth. He shot her a glare before opening his mouth to no doubt scold me. I fumbled for my phone and flashed the screen at him. He stopped in his tracks, and concentrated on my get out of jail free card.

"I really am sorry, I meant no harm."

Nodding his head slowly, he turned to walk away but not before gracing me with a parting shot that I had heard more times than I could count. "I suggest seeing a doctor young lady."

Wow, why hadn't I thought of that? Perry had been patiently standing beside me, letting me handle the situation as I had already told him to do but it was obviously too much for him.

"Listen arsehole..."

I dragged him away, sharing an apologetic look with the rude man's daughter before he could get us thrown out.

163

"It's fine."

"No, it fucking isn't," Perry growled, eyes still focused on the man.

Sighing, I pulled him down into a seat at the table and wished for the night to be over. Of course, Simone was relentless in wanting to know what had happened, Daniel fought my corner and told her to let it go... and I remembered why I chose not to put myself in these situations in the first place.

"What does it say on your phone?"

I passed it over to Jason and busied myself looking at the drinks menu. I didn't tend to have much in the way of alcohol because, well, I liked to try to be in control as much as possible when I had the chance, but I felt like tonight I was going to need it.

"This is brilliant," Jason laughed, passing it around the table. "I might have to get something like that."

"What do you need to share with the world? Everyone knows you're an idiot already," Annie laughed.

"I could use it to fight off all the women that come onto me. Firefighters are sexy you know," he confided.

She shrugged as if this all made perfect sense.

"Dan has one on his phone too," Jasmine piped up. "It says *Annoying bastard that doesn't understand personal space.*"

"No it doesn't, it says *will strip for money*," Simone laughed.

"More like, Prolonged staring at this sexy specimen will cause your knickers to combust." Daniel declared proudly.

164

"Gross," Annie muttered.

"Disgusting," Jasmine quipped, her face scrunching up like she had smelt something bad.

"*Pizda*," I choked out, my eyes widening.

Simone burst out laughing, her hand slapping at the table as Daniel gasped indignantly.

"Did she just call me a cu..."

"Can I take your drink orders?"

Saved by the waitress in black. I just hoped the rest of the night was less... Willow.

26 – Breaking the rules

Perry

"Does anyone have any questions?"

I glanced around the room and couldn't help the grin that spread across my face. It was a huge day for the Gold Dime Group. We had finally finished with the marketing aspect for our new tech line and today we were pitching to the big wigs at all the leading internet and mobile providers in the UK, hoping that they would pick the line up. Not that there was any chance they would decline, especially as we had bagged the number one just this morning.

Still, it was a thrill to see all our hard work combined into a neat little package and presented. Especially when it was my girlfriend up there talking through the marketing. She had been a nervous wreck up until today, scared to death that her nerves would get the best of her but from the moment she had stood up and started to talk, she had been nothing short of perfection.

I couldn't be prouder of her. Jasmine and Ben were smiling and nodding their encouragement throughout, but she didn't once look in their direction for comfort. Nope, my girl looked at me when she needed to, and didn't that just make me feel like puffing my chest out.

Jasmine had taken centre stage for now and Willow was able to take a seat opposite me, a slight flush to her skin but a smile on her face. She was breath-taking. I was on the verge of dragging her out of there and finding the nearest cupboard when I was called upon to pitch the last of the presentation.

I could feel her eyes on me the whole time, watching my every move. She was cataloguing the way I held myself, the pauses I took between sentences... anything she could to help her if she needed to do this again in the future.

Seemed like a much better strategy than stripping to me.

Even the thought of it made me violent. There was no way my girl was getting up on a stage like that again, not while I was breathing. Although, I wouldn't be opposed to a private showing. Those long curvy legs. That corset. Those glorious huge breasts...

It was about this time that I realised two things:

The presentation was over, and we could leave.

And that I was about to debrief Willow in my office – with my cock.

✓✓✓

"Was it ok? It felt ok."

"Uh huh."

"I was nervous, and I couldn't help the hand flexing, but I think it actually helped that I wasn't focusing so hard on not trying to tic."

"Uh huh."

She glanced back at me as I ushered her off the elevator in record time and practically dragged her through the hallway to our department.

"Is there a fire I don't know about," she

laughed.

I didn't answer, I couldn't. I just knew that I had to get her alone. Our floor was quiet since most of the staff were at lunch, so nobody noticed us bombing through the door of my office. The second the door was closed and locked, I was on her.

She gasped as I grabbed her arse, lifted her onto my desk and attacked her mouth with abandon. But that wasn't enough, and I was about to break my promise of keeping things professional in the workplace.

Did I give a fuck?

"Perry," she moaned quietly, head thrown back as I nipped my way down her throat.

"You were fucking amazing in there," I groaned.

The buttons on her blouse gave way and I was rewarded with the heavy mounds of her breasts, barely contained as she panted. With more gentleness that I thought I possessed, I pulled the cups down and captured a nipple between my teeth.

Her legs gripped my hips, her skirt bunching around the tops of her thighs. She looked wanton.

"Ohhh," she breathed when I stepped back and took her lacy briefs with me. A coy smile spread across her luscious mouth and the next thing I knew she was on her knees before me and my cock had jumped from horny to desperate.

She didn't waste any time. My trousers were open and my shaft in her mouth faster than I could say *that's a moist bird.*

"Willow," I began but she chose that moment

to take me deep into the back of her throat and I swear I blacked out for a moment.

I came back to reality when she left me hanging, rose to her feet and backed away.

"Where the hell are you going?" I moved closer, but she kept backing up, a mischievous little grin on her face as she rounded the desk.

"I've had this little fantasy in my head for weeks now..."

I watched as she pulled my chair out and gave a nod for me to sit down. Loving the fact that her ideas worked with my own, I dropped down onto the leather and watched as Willow pulled her skirt further up around her hips. The sight of her pussy right in front of me was enough to make my mouth water.

I grabbed a hold of her arse once again and hoisted her onto the desk in front of me.

"Wait, that wasn't..." she began but I wasn't stopping for anyone.

"I believe you told me to nibble your giblets Miss Summers."

She groaned and covered her face. "Thanks for reminding me."

My hands grasped at her thighs, spread them wide and then I feasted. It was more than a thrill, it was the sexiest thing I had ever seen. My girl spread out on my desk, her feet propped up on the arms of my chair and those killer fucking heels she always wore for work digging into my sides.

I couldn't get enough of her, couldn't seem to touch enough of her as one hand reached up for her face and the other snuck between her legs, wanting to get in on the action. My eyes rose to see her reaction when two fingers slipped inside

169

just in time to see her grab my hand and place my thumb in her mouth.

And that ladies and gentlemen is how my restraint broke and Willow found herself bouncing up and down on my cock in the middle of the day, in my office... with her hand clamped over my mouth because I couldn't stop telling her to fuck me hard – loudly.

My hands were gripped on her arse as she rode me like a bronco, her tits bouncing in my face with too much speed to catch one with my mouth. It was like being teased and pleased all at the same time. I could feel my balls beginning to tighten way too quickly for my liking, so I upped the ante, snuck a hand back between us and went for gold.

She bucked above me, her motions getting frantic as I massaged her clit in time to the pounding of my heart. I could feel her clamping around my shaft and I doubled my efforts, needing her to go over before I did. She shuddered, her thighs strained, and I could feel deep in my soul the moment she let go. Her face slackened, her mouth formed the perfect 'o' and she had never looked more beautiful.

One, two, three thrusts of my hips and I was right there with her. Although I'd wager my life savings, her 'o' face was a lot fucking prettier than mine. She collapsed onto my chest, her body still shaking and mine trying to calm the fuck down. For someone who was in decent shape, I was doing a good impression of an unfit bastard.

"That was..."

"Fuck," I groaned against her hair. "That was fucking epic."

170

She giggled and right then and there, it became my favourite sound in the world. Apart from her moans that is. Or maybe her sighs... fuck it. Every sound Willow made was my favourite.

Yes, again I know... pussy whipped.

"Kocham cie," she blurted and immediately stiffened in my arms.

I chuckled quietly. "Are you swearing at me in polish again babe."

She burrowed into my chest and let out a shaky breath. "Something like that."

27 - Blame it on the boogie

Willow

I sank further into the cushions and pretended to listen to my cousin as she talked about the devastation her kitchen had become. It was Daniels night to cook and that never ended well. Usually I looked forward to these talks because they always ended in disaster and nothing made me laugh more than Daniel looking like a chump.

Tonight however, I was struggling to even focus on the words flowing down the phone. I was still on a high from the presentation I had successfully managed to give today. Then of course was the earth shattering sexcapades in Perry's office... I blushed even thinking about it.

All of that was paling in the face of my epic slip of the Tourette's challenged tongue.

'Kocham cie' I had mumbled, totally out of the blue while I came down from the mother of all orgasms. I was used to random polish floating past my lips, it didn't happen very often but enough for it to be expected from my nearest and dearest. It was the first time I had ever muttered those words though.

I love you.

It was all I had been able to think about since. I had shrugged it off and let him think it meant whatever he wanted... because I wasn't ready to address it. Just because I wasn't ready, didn't mean I was stupid. I knew immediately, before the final syllable had passed my lips that:

A – Owen may have a point about vocal tics

being relevant to the situation; we'll never hear the end of this.

B – I was in love with Perry Moore.

It didn't even come as a surprise... which is surprising. I know, I'm a walking contradiction. All I know is, it felt natural. Not the tic, that always feels like a natural thing to do that shouldn't be happening. No this was different. When he asked if I was swearing at him, it was on the tip of my tongue to tell him straight.

But I wasn't ready... was I? It was too soon. Wasn't it?

I managed to tune back in to the one-sided conversation Simone was having long enough to say goodnight without her calling me out on ignoring her. I just hoped I hadn't agreed to anything. Last time I zoned out on a call with her, I found myself with two little girls on my doorstep at 7am on a Sunday morning and no clue why.

It was early still, and I was feeling restless. I didn't think I would settle and there was no way I was going to concentrate enough to cook, so I chucked on my boots and opted to walk down to the Thai restaurant a few streets over. The beauty of living on the outskirts of town was that the world was quite literally on my doorstep. Which was handy when I was carless.

Stepping out into the street, I could feel my head start to relax. It was a clear night, a slight chill to the air but perfect for taking a wander. Within ten minutes I was walking through the door of Thai Delights and being greeted warmly by Cho behind the bar. I had been coming here for a while now and they were used to me. New situations tended to make first meetings memorable with me, and that had been the case here for sure.

She passed me a soft drink on the house, told me to take a seat while she got my order ready and was already buzzing about the room before I could say thank you. I was just sitting down in the waiting area when I heard a familiar voice. Glancing up, I stilled when I saw perfectly styled blond hair and enough gold to start a mine.

Amelia hadn't seen me thank goodness. I shrunk back and tried to hide myself behind the huge potted plant native to these restaurants. I could hear her whining to her dinner partner and couldn't help the roll of my eyes. She was high maintenance if ever I saw it. Who in their right mind would want to date that?

Then she stepped back, and I nearly died laughing. It was Perry's brother, Archie, looking bored to tears and far too busy eyeing up the menu to pay attention to the shrew.

"You're not even listening to me, are you?"

"Not really babe," he drawled.

I hid my snigger.

"For god sake. You said you would find something on that half-breed. He's still dating her you know."

Now that had my ears pricking up. Were they talking about me?

"Give it up already. He's never going to date you, let alone marry you." Archie leant in and placed a hand on her arse. "It's about time you gave in."

"I am not marrying you Archibald."

"So you keep saying."

"Look," she crooned, slipping closer to him and batting her eyes at his frowning face. "You know how particular my trust fund is. I need to marry the first born and it must be a family of prestige. Nothing would change Archie. We'd still have this."

Her hand shot out and palmed an area I had no intention of looking at. My ears stayed fully alert though. This was by far the most fascinating conversation I had ever heard. What kind of people put conditions and clauses on love? *Scratch that,* I thought. This had nothing to do with love, this was all about the money.

Damn it, I should have recorded this for Perry. Even he wasn't sure why Amelia was so dead set on getting her hooks into him, especially since she was sleeping with his brother.

"Willow! Your order ready." Cho called out in her broken English.

Oh shit. Grimacing, I got to my feet and thanked Cho, not daring to look over and see if they had clocked me. Not that it mattered because I would have to walk past them to get out of the building and there was no way I could stall now. Why couldn't they have been seated already? Bad Cho.

I kept my head down and had nearly drawn level with them when a pair of stunning black heels stood in my way. FYI, owning those gorgeous heels was enough reason for me to hate her, the rest was just the icing.

"Willow, how lovely to see you again." She made a show of looking around me. "Dear, are you allowed out without a carer?"

"Jesus, could you be any more of a bitch? No

wonder Perry has never wanted you."

I tried to move past her, but she slid to the right and stepped in a little closer. "Were you eavesdropping on us?"

I stepped back and appraised her. Was she worried? She sure looked like it. "It was kinda hard to ignore I'm afraid. You're very loud."

Her lips twisted into a sneer. "How dare you. If you so much as breath a word of this to anyone I'll make you rue the day you met your precious boyfriend."

Did she just threaten me? Oh hell no. I was opening my mouth, ready to give her a taste of her own medicine when Cho popped up out of nowhere.

"Miss? Your table is ready for you now."

She straightened and plastered a fake smile on her face. "Thank you so much. Would you make sure my friend gets outside safely please? She has mental health issues you know."

She walked off, Archie trailing slowly behind her while I wished for the perfect comeback that just wouldn't come. A group of ladies that had been waiting in line looked at me with a mix of sympathetic and curious eyes. Of course, I was giving them something to look at as my trademark shoulder and hand tics came out in force.

I flashed my screen saver at them, not even bothering to offer the usual smile or shrug. At this point, I couldn't care less what they thought of me, I was too busy seething inside at the walking ignoramus. I would never understand how someone could be so unbelievably rude and uncaring towards another human being. Holding my head high, I

176

walked around the queue and made a move for the door.

"Willow?"

Cho caught up to me and held the door. "You no worry. We all spit in the bitch's food."

I chuckled and gave her arm a pat. "Thank you, that's brilliantly evil."

"Even better," she winked. "I have cold."

28 – It isn't what it looks like

Perry

"Are you gonna answer that?"

I shoved my phone over to the nosy woman and carried on eating my omelette.

"Oh, I see," Annie laughed, tapping her nose, ever the conspirator. "Ignoring the parentals again are we."

I shrugged as I chewed and tried not to feel guilty. It had been weeks since that fateful night we had dinner together. Usually by now I would throw them a call or at the least a text to let them know I was still alive, but this time was different. I needed them to know that I meant business.

Didn't mean I felt good about it though. I loved my parents, but this was important to me, Willow was important to me and I needed to make that clear right from the start. I hadn't read a single text, listened to a single voicemail or answered any of the hundreds of calls my mother had made. I had even told the switchboard at work to tell them I was on a conference call and couldn't be interrupted if they intercepted a call from them.

Sad but true. I was boycotting the Moore's and I felt like a total twat for it. I hadn't even told Willow just to what extent I had taken things because I knew she would make me talk to them. She didn't want to come between us even though I had told her time and again that there wasn't much of a relationship between my folks and I in the first place. She was adamant that I try to make amends with them, citing that she knew what it was like to be without parents and I should do my best to make things right.

"Have you even heard them out yet?"

I narrowed my eyes at my best friend. "What's with the third degree?"

She crossed her arms, totally unfazed by my glare. "Answer the question dumbass!"

"No, I haven't."

"You're an idiot."

I shot her the finger and jumped up to leave the table. "And you're a bitch."

She laughed and took my plate from me, not offended in the least. "Why thank you."

It stayed on my mind as I cleaned my teeth and finally made it out the door. It stayed there right the way through until I parked outside Willow's apartment building and left the motor running. Was I being too harsh?

She breezed into my car and leant over to peck my cheek.

"What the hell kind of greeting is that?"

Her face screwed up adorably. "Huh? I thought it would be ok, it's not like we're outside the office or anything."

I shushed her with my lips – the way it should be done. Passionate, full on, sexy as fuck. She looked dazed when I finished greeting her properly and didn't that just make me feel fucking awesome.

"Oh," she whispered, a small smile on those rosy lips.

"Oh, she says," I dropped another kiss to her mouth and helped her snap her seatbelt in place. "If all I'm getting is *oh*, I need to up my game."

She giggled, my favourite sound (yeah, I

know, we've covered this already) and settled back into her seat as I pulled away from the curb.

"So, I had an interesting night."

"Yeah?"

She fidgeted in her seat and it took me a moment to notice she was fisting her hands in her lap. "Why are you holding back?"

She glanced over to me and back to her hands. "Sorry."

I frowned. "Don't be sorry. I just thought we were at the stage where you were comfortable enough around me. I don't like the fact that you concentrate so hard on suppressing your tics all day at work as it is. I don't want you doing that with me too."

"Pull over," she demanded.

Worried that there was something wrong, I swerved the car into a layby and immediately turned to make sure she was ok. She pounced.

Her arms wrapped around my neck and she mashed her lips against mine furiously. I groaned at her attack, more than willing to let her have her way with me. Sadly, she pulled back all too soon and left me dazed, grinning and saluting her in my pants.

"What was that for?"

"You know. Just for accepting me, warts and all."

"Hey now, I didn't say shit about warts. That's a deal breaker!"

She giggled and pressed her lips back to mine, this time without the urgency. If anything, it made my dick harder. With a deep sigh, and a quick trouser adjustment that had her grinning coyly out the window, we were

180

back on the road and heading to work.

We were both so lost in our thoughts that it didn't occur to me until much later when I was knee deep in conference calls that she never did tell me what had happened last night.

✔✔✔

"To that end, I want to thank you all for your hard work over the last few weeks. We have a long road ahead of us now, but the path is clear, and I think I speak for both Max and myself when I say you've done us and the Gold Dime Group proud."

Jasmine stood from the head of the conference table and smiled at us all. It was a packed room with most of my team in here at her insistence. The feedback from the presentations had been astounding and we were expecting to have a huge chunk of the mobile phone market in our corner over the next few weeks. There was still a lot of fine tuning to be done but for the most part, my section was done.

Jasmine flitted about, giving everyone a little praise as she went, and I confessed to be a little in awe of how much attention she seemed to pay to her employees. I mean, *I* knew what my staff had contributed, even the little things like Martha suggesting the gold trim on one of the banners, but the fact that the big boss knew that? Mind blowing.

We were just starting to pack up when the door opened and a very flustered Tina from reception poked her head around the door. All

181

eyes turned to her and if it was even possible, her face turned a deeper shade of red than her hair.

"I'm sorry to interrupt but I need Mr Moore."

And now all eyes turned to me. "Can it wait Tina, we're just finishing up."

She wrung her hands in front of her and looked like she was going to be sick. "Um, not really."

Jasmine sighed and crossed her arms over her chest. "What could possibly be so important that you need him right now?"

Poor Tina paled further, and I was starting to feel a little uneasy. "Mr Moore has a visitor in his office. It's quite urgent."

"Who?" A million thoughts flew through my head in that split second. Was there something wrong with Annie? With my parents?

Tina's eyes darted to Willow and I swear I saw sympathy. What the hell was going on?

"It's your fiancé, Mr Moore."

Stunned, I turned to the room waiting for someone to tell me I had heard wrong but by the judging looks and the horror on my girlfriend's face, that wasn't going to happen.

"I don't have a fiancé."

"She was quite insistent," Tina continued and from the tone of her voice, so clipped and annoyed I knew there was only one person it could be.

Muttering under my breath, I pushed through the door and stormed down to the elevator, ready to tear the bitch a new arsehole for turning up here like this. Who the hell did she think she was? Hadn't I made it as clear as possible that there was never going to be anything between us? This was a new low, even for her.

My rage had reached epic proportions by the time I slammed my way into my office. But what I wasn't expecting was to find Amelia crying silently while she leant against my desk and looking as miserable as she could be.

"I'm so sorry for lying about who I was but I needed to see you and didn't think that lady would let me in otherwise."

I closed the door but didn't make a move. I wasn't sure what was happening here, but I wasn't taking my eyes off the conniving woman. "What was so important that you had to give my entire office the impression that I'm a cheating bastard?"

Her face blanched and the surprise was plain to see. She was shocked that everyone knew I was with Willow. "I didn't even think about that. God, she must hate me even more now."

Rolling my eyes, I walked to my chair and dropped down, steepling my fingers in front of me on the desk. "Spill it Amelia, I haven't got all day."

"My grandad is dying."

My heart stopped for one beat and all the irritation drained out of me. "Shit Amelia, I'm so sorry."

She nodded and started rummaging around in her handbag for a tissue. I had a lot of time for William, her grandfather. He was an astounding man, been there, seen it and done it all. He was the one that told me to be true to myself and forge my own way in life, not just blindly follow in my father's footsteps. He was always larger than life, I couldn't imagine anything taking him down.

Amelia was still searching in that colossal bag of hers, so I took pity and grabbed the box off my desk, walking it round to her. I wasn't a heartless bastard after all. "Here."

"Thank you," she whimpered, immediately breaking down into tears again and throwing herself at me.

It was awkward. I patted her probably much too hard on the back and I think I even mumbled *there there* like I was talking to a toddler. She pulled back and looked at me with glassy eyes and I could've kicked myself for not seeing her intentions quickly enough. She planted her lips on mine and practically forced her tongue into my mouth before I twigged what was happening.

I pushed her away roughly and swiped a hand over my mouth. All I could see was red lipstick all over my palm. "What the fuck was that?"

"I thought we were having a moment?" She looked genuinely confused and I couldn't help the giant laugh that boomed from my chest.

"Are you fucking kidding me? We will never, and I mean never, have *a moment*. I'm tired of having this conversation with you. It's never going to happen."

"But, I've been saving myself for you Perry. You're the one."

She made a bid to step closer, but I held a hand up, nearly clocking her in the face and she stumbled back. "This is pathetic. For one, you've been making the beast with two backs with Archie for years."

She gasped and held a hand to her chest,

ready to deny the charges but I was so done with this shit. "Don't even try it. He sends me pictures and videos all the damn time. Do you have any idea how wrong it is to see your brothers cock thrusting away every time I stupidly open an attachment?"

Her eyes narrowed but she wisely kept her mouth shut.

"And two, it's a new low, even for you to use your grandfathers condition as an excuse to get what you want."

"You bastard," she seethed but I was beyond giving a shit what she thought.

"Now I'll say this one more time, so pay attention. It's never going to happen. Stay the fuck away from me and Willow and every fucking aspect of our lives, or you'll regret it."

Her eyebrows raised in disbelief. "Threatening me now?"

"Just giving you a friendly warning."

"I came here for a shoulder to cry on and this is how you treat me?"

"No," I shook my head sadly and rounded my desk. "You came here because you knew it would hurt Willow. Now get the fuck out of my office."

She stood and made a show of straightening her jacket. "If you had a heart, you wouldn't treat me this way."

I laughed. "If *you* had a heart, you wouldn't be making a play for your lover's brother."

She grabbed the heavy stapler off the corner and threw it with all her might in my direction and that was the moment I thanked the universe for giving me lightning reflexes. It sailed past my ear and crashed into the wall

185

with a loud thud.

She didn't wait to be told to get the fuck out again.

Best decision she'd made all day.

Within seconds I had my mobile in hand and pressed to my ear. He may be a complete idiot, but I couldn't keep this shit from my brother.

"Did hell freeze over?"

"Close enough. Your booty call just made one hell of a scene at my office."

He sighed and listened to the sorry tale. I expected him to jump to her defence like he normally did but instead, he laughed. "William isn't dying, he just has high cholesterol!"

"You're kidding me!" Stunned, I sat back. Although I didn't know why this should surprise me, the woman was a manipulative bitch.

"True story. I'd have paid big money to see her face when you told her I had videos. Comedy fucking gold!"

"Jesus, you're as tapped in the head as she is."

"No," he drawled. "I'm just loving the fact that we both put her in her place within 24 hours. I bet she feels ridiculous right now."

"What do you mean?"

"Well, last night I realised that she was never going to give me an actual chance. I'm not important enough to be her partner, just her bit on the side."

I frowned. "I would have thought that would suit you?"

He chuckled humorously. "You really don't know me at all do you? I haven't so much as looked at another woman for the last 7 years, hoping that she would take our relationship seriously. I want a family while I'm still young enough to enjoy them. I thought she was the one, but all she really cares about, even now is money."

"Shit Archie, I had no idea."

"Well you wouldn't would you. We never talk."

What was that burning sensation deep in my gut. Fucking guilt.

"Mate..."

"It's all good. Between her catty remarks about me not being acceptable as a husband and the way she treated Willow, I'm done."

"Yeah she was a complete bitch that night at Mum's."

"Yeah, she was, and Willow seems great. She didn't deserve that. But I meant the showdown between them last night actually."

I paused for a beat. "What?"

"Last night at *Thai Delights*. She was a complete cow, Willow held her own though."

I pinched the bridge of my nose and took a deep breath against the unease I could feel building.

"Archie, I think you need to start at the beginning!"

29 – She started it

Willow

Have you ever felt like you were on a stage, under a spotlight and every pair of eyes for miles were on you? I understand how people may like the feeling, hell I'd quite enjoyed it for a little when I took my turn at Hot Steppers.

Here and now however? It was absolutely the worst feeling. My colleagues were watching me, some giggled nervously like they weren't sure what I was going to do. Others had sad or angry looks on their faces. I didn't have a clue what emotions I was displaying.

I was embarrassed, hurt, disappointed and above all angry. But not at Perry. He couldn't be held accountable for the crazy workings of that woman's mind but Jesus, when was she going to get the message?

"Ok, I think we've had enough drama for one day," Jasmine called out to the crowd. "Thanks for your time everyone, you can leave now and please keep in mind that this is a business, not a schoolyard. Act like the responsible, sensible adults we're paying you to be."

One by one they filed out of the conference room, some glancing my way while others tried to look everywhere but straight at me. I noticed Owen hold back, a furious set to his shoulders and a little defeated sigh escaped my lips.

"Just wait here for a minute Will," Jasmine whispered as she breezed past me. She started hurrying the lurkers and it wasn't until the last one left and she closed the door that I let out a thundering groan.

"That chicken needs plucking and don't be gentle."

"Plucking? That chicken needs fucking throttling!" Owen grumbled, then blanched when he realised it wasn't just me and him in the room.

Jasmine smiled and gave him a little salute. "Couldn't have said it better myself."

Looking relieved, he turned his attention to me. "That was bollocks, you *know* that right?"

"Of course I do, she's crazy."

He gestured to my out of control shoulder. "You need to calm down a little."

I gave him a withering look and dropped into the nearest chair. "Yeah, I'll get right on that, thanks for the advice."

He wisely chose to keep his mouth shut after that, instead he just elected to stand against the wall and mutter about how some woman should be locked up from the moment they became women. It all sounded a little barbaric to me, but it was a great distraction from my body's total meltdown.

That was potentially a little dramatic. But I felt like I was being pulled in two directions from the inside, my limbs felt tingly, almost as if I was about to get a full body case of pins and needles. It was intense, strange and although I was lucky to only go through the imminent body struggle a couple of times a month, I still felt so helplessly out of control every time.

I was on the verge of having a ticcing fit. I could feel my body's urges beginning to take over, not just the normal shrugs and flexes that my mild condition subjected me to. No this was going to be much worse and it was going to

189

scare the hell out of Jasmine and Owen.

Slipping from the chair, I positioned myself away from harm as best I could and took a deep breath.

"Owen, please stay for a minute."

He looked confused and dropped down onto the floor beside me. "Willow, what's going on?"

Jasmine crouched down next to him, concern etched over her face.

"Tic... tic... fit..."

And that was as far as I got. Owen caught my head before it could hit the ground, I would have to remember to thank him for that when this was over. Jasmine watched on, tears in her eyes as my body became something separate from me, a will and mind of its own as it twisted and wrenched. All my favourite tics, and some that hadn't been a problem since childhood all came out in full force and there was absolutely nothing I could do to stop it.

I couldn't talk. I couldn't tell them that I was still here in mind. I couldn't tell them with words that I was ok, hurting and aching, but ok. To the outside world, it looked like a body possession, something that you would see in a horror flick. On the inside, it was like being trapped inside someone else's body.

My torso cramped up, dragging my body into a ball and twisting in such a way I thought my hip would dislocate. It felt so tight in my own skin, even though the work out I was getting really should have made everything feel limber.

Owen sat patiently beside me and watched my hands, my feet, my face intermittently, looking for a sign that I was ok. He had witnessed several tic attacks from the kids at the drop-in centre. Lucky for me, he knew that if it didn't go on for too long, I would be just fine immediately after. It was more traumatising for those witnessing than the ones having the seizure.

I managed to throw a wink at him, followed by a brief reprieve in my left hand so that I could snap my fingers. He blew out a shaky breath and mumbled to Jasmine that I was doing fine.

"What's happening to her?"

He explained patiently to her, his eyes never leaving my eyes or my hand now that he knew what to look out for. She wrung her hands in her lap and nodded along as he told her everything was going to be just fine.

"What if it goes on for too long?"

"I've never seen her have one before. They can last anything from a few minutes to an hour, so it's difficult to judge. But Willow has a mild diagnosis with complex vocal tics, she generally doesn't display many motor tics, so I wouldn't allow this to go on for longer than ten minutes."

My eye shut and reopened briefly, the only way I could let him know that I agreed with him. Six minutes was the longest I had gone. I didn't want to waste anyone's time needlessly.

For what felt like forever, I lay on the floor of that room, grateful for Jasmine's attempts to keep my skirt from showing too much skin and even more thankful for Owen's watchful eye. I could feel the control slowly starting to return to me, in tiny increments. The movements began to slow, became less exaggerated. My head and neck finally stilled from the slow roll it had been doing throughout the ordeal.

Eventually my stomach relaxed enough to give my spine and hips a reprieve from the repeated crunching. My foot stopped jerking and then, all was quiet.

I heard Owen mumble to Jasmine before ducking out of the room. I closed my eyes and concentrated on my breathing for a few beats, just wanting to be sure it was truly over. Rustling reached my ears, and then I was being helped into a sitting position. Owen held a straw to my mouth and ordered me to take a sip.

The juice slipped down, refreshing my parched throat. I glanced over to them both apologetically and Jasmine shook her head firmly.

"If you so much as whisper the words *I'm sorry*, I'll fire your fucking arse!"

✔✔✔

"I don't need to go home, honestly."

"I bloody do, that was crazy."

Jasmine and I both scowled at Owen who just shrugged and pushed his way passed us. "Just saying!"

"Thanks again," I yelled but he just waved it off like he had the first ten times I had said it.

"He was amazing you know," Jasmine confided as we walked to the elevator. "If he wasn't brilliant right where he is, I would be pushing him to pursue a career as a paramedic."

"You should see him in action at the centre.

Everyone loves him there."

She linked her arm through mine. "He'd make a great boyfriend too."

I shrugged. "He would. Problem is, he's a total commitment phobe."

"Really? You surprise me."

"Yup, the idea of settling down, wife and kids etc, makes him shudder. Its mental."

I hitched my bag over my shoulder, courtesy of the man in question and tried to tell the boss yet again that I was completely fine and didn't need to go home.

"Look," she pushed the button for the ground level. "It's going to be tough to walk back into that office right now. I don't know if Perry is still dealing with the imposter. You've had a rough day and I'm afraid I have to insist that you get the hell out of here."

We reached the bottom and she practically ushered me out the door. "Is that why you're manhandling me as if I've been caught stealing paper clips."

She gasped. "It's always the quiet ones."

"You!"

We both turned mid laugh and came face to face with the snooty cow herself. She had panda eyes although there wasn't an ounce of sadness about her, only anger. She stalked from the door of the ladies' room and closed the distance between us in seconds.

"How dare you steal my fiancé. What kind of person are you?"

If I had thought it was embarrassing before, now it was downright humiliating. More than twenty sets of eyes stopped what they were doing and turned to gawk at us.

"I'm not getting involved in this. He's told you time and again there's nothing between you..."

She laughed humourlessly. "Well of course that's what he would say to you. Did you even bother to question why I was about all the time? Just how naïve are you?"

About all the time? Was she being serious right now? "I've literally met you twice."

"Just because you're *'mentally handicapped'*," she quipped, making the air quote sign with her fingers. "It doesn't give you the right to steal other women's men."

You could have heard a pin drop in the room. And it was a seriously big room.

"I suggest you leave now or I'll have you removed." Jasmine seethed beside me, phone in hand and ready to put her threat into action.

Amelia held her hands up. "I understand, you have a duty of care towards the disabled employees."

I was fast losing my patience with this idiot. "Oh my god, would you listen to yourself? You don't have a clue what you're talking about do you?"

"I'm sorry, was that not the pc term?" she glanced around as if asking for help. "Retarded? Nope, mentally challenged. Mentally impaired..."

"That's it, get the hell out of my building now Amelia."

That got the woman's attention. "Excuse me?"

"Oh, that's right," Jasmine remarked, tapping out a message on her phone. She finished her task and faced Amelia. "I know exactly who you are. I also know exactly who your father is. I believe in fact, he relies quite heavily on the work he does for this company. I wonder what he would think of your behaviour today."

"I didn't... wait..." Amelia stammered as two burly men in black suits drew up on either side of her. Genuine fear spread across her features as Jasmine hitched a thumb towards the door.

"Gentlemen, please escort this woman from the building."

They each took an arm and dragged the squirming, pleading woman towards the doors. Silence followed, weighed with unspoken questions and probing stares. They knew. They knew something wasn't quite right about me. It didn't matter that the woman had seemed kinda crazy or that she was thrown from the building by the boss.

I hadn't been able to outright refute her allegations because, well, I did have a disability. I wasn't going to lie about it, I had never been asked before, so it had been easy to avoid.

But now?

"On seconds thought, maybe a half-day would do me good."

30 – The fight of my life

Perry

Stepping from the office should have been an easy task but not when you had a group of hostile faces aimed at you. That bitch had managed to ruin my reputation in less than five minutes.

I couldn't see Willow anywhere and she was the only person I was concerned about. I hoped she had stayed in the conference room so that's where I was heading but I didn't get more than a few steps when Owen tackled me back into the office.

"Is she ok?"

He closed the door and started pacing the floor. "I'm gonna say this once…"

"I swear to you, she's a crazy, delusional bitch."

He relaxed a little and leant back against the door, arms crossed. "I figured. Willow didn't buy it for a second."

Thank god. "Doesn't excuse it though does it. Now we have a whole building of people thinking I'm a womaniser."

He chuckled mirthlessly. "Well yeah, but I would be more concerned about what effect this has just had on Will."

"What do you mean?"

He pushed away and pulled out a chair for me. "You'd better take a seat."

Every word that met my ears had my heart breaking. She had suffered because of the drama being with me had caused. I knew she wouldn't see it that way, but it didn't make me feel any better. I needed to find her.

"Mrs Hope made her go home."

That was all I needed to hear. I was out of my seat and throwing my door open only to be stopped in my tracks again. This time, by my boss. Jasmine stood in the hallway, a fierce look on her face that had my balls shrivelling up. I suddenly understood what Annie had been talking about.

"We need to talk Mr Moore."

I stared at the clock for the umpteenth time and scowled. It was nearly 9pm and I was parked outside Willow's apartment block. I'd been there for over 2 hours, staring up at her dark windows and generally looking like a stalker. I didn't care.

I didn't know where else to look. I came straight here when I left the Gold Dime Group earlier, and that had been hours ago. When I was sure she wasn't here, I tried Simone's, the park, her favourite coffee shop but she was nowhere to be seen. I even went to the arcades on a whim but there was no sight of her.

I'd had to explain the whole ordeal to her cousin – who cried, then screamed, then slapped me so hard I saw stars. I welcomed the punishment. I understood deep down that I hadn't done anything wrong but fuck if it didn't feel like it was all my fault.

My phone had been blowing up all afternoon. Worried texts and calls from Annie, Jason, Jasmine, Ben, Owen... but not Daniel Hope. He had been strangely silent. Now call me suspicious but he and Willow were as tight as siblings, and if he wasn't busting my arse, I figured he knew where she was. It was a thought I held onto, anything to stop the panic that was threatening to take over.

I daren't leave in case she came back, but I knew she wasn't going to. I rang Simone again, annoyed when the line clicked over to voicemail. I wanted to believe she would tell me if there was something I needed to know but how could I be sure. Instead I left a message and tried my best to not lose my temper.

Where was she? I just wanted to hold her, touch her, tell her how sorry I was for all this shit that had invaded her life. She was the best thing that ever happened to me and the thought that I could lose her was making me crazy. I vowed then and there that I would do whatever it took to make this right. I'd file a lawsuit against Amelia, quit my job, disown my family once and for all if it helped. Anything.

My phoned chimed once again and I grabbed for it in a panic, desperately hoping it would be my girl.

"It's me," my brother said, and my heart sank.

"Hey."

"Did you find her?"

"How did you know…"

"I went to Annie's to see you."

Well. I didn't know what to say to that. "I bet that was interesting."

He laughed. "She slapped me, jabbed her finger into my chest. Shouted at me. Called me some of the most inventive names in the history of man... then she hugged me, introduced me to Jason and fuck man, it was like no time had passed at all."

That was Annie all right. Back in the day, the three of us had been inseparable. It only changed when we all went off to different universities. Annie stayed local, going to the Reading U and me and Archie ended up at Harvard. Where I kept in contact with her and met up with her as often as I could, Archie got a case of asshole that stayed with him for a long time. Luckily it wasn't contagious.

"I don't know where else to look Archie."

He sighed. "Hang on, I'm nearly there."

The phone went dead just as a Taxi pulled up on the other side of the road. My brother jumped out and made his way over to the side of the car. I was touched he would make the effort, didn't mean I was getting out of the car though. I settled for winding the window down, eyes still watching her apartment like a hawk.

"You sure she isn't being hidden from you? I mean, her cousin is hardly going to take your side in all of this. Not that you've done anything wrong, but you know what I mean."

I shook my head solemnly. "I don't know Archie."

He watched me for a moment then stood abruptly, slapping the side of the car. "Come on, this isn't doing you any good. She isn't gonna come back here tonight. I say we go and get shit faced."

Groaning, I rubbed my hands down my face. "No offence, that is the worst idea I've ever heard."

His eyebrows raised, and a smirk marred his

mouth. "It beats sitting here, pining away and looking like a stalker."

Damn it, he had me there.

"Fuck it... lead the way brother."

✔✔✔

There was no denying it... I was drunk. I mean, it wasn't like I had many other explanations for why I was stumbling down the street, no shoes on and was struggling to focus on the man in front of me. Archie veered to the left so of course I followed him. He was after all my big brother.

"You see... love is for pussy's."

He was just so wise. "You're just saying that because you fell for a twat."

"She is a twat!" he raised his arms to the air and shouted, "Amelia is a twat!"

My face broke out into a huge grin as the laughter exploded from me. He looked ridiculous.

"So Perry, what's the plan?"

I caught his arm and tried to steer him round the parked car. Then a bush came out of nowhere and attacked my legs. Arms flailing, I fell backwards, flat on my back and legs in the air. Silence echoed around until Archie's boyish giggle wafted over. I tried to pull myself out, but it just wasn't happening. I needed to get out of here, I had places to be. A person to see.

"Fucking help me then!"

He crawled over on his hands and knees, tears running down his face. When did he fall over? "I know you're desperate for bush but really Reginald?"

Oh no he didn't. "Watch it Archibald!"

He scowled, at least I think that was the look he was going for and dived right into the prickly bush with me. The breath whooshed out of my lungs as the big oaf landed on top of me and then I landed a perfectly timed uppercut to his nose.

He howled and reared back, fists flying while my legs kicked at him to get the bastard off me. It was an epic fight of perfect form and I felt sure if there were any MMA scouts here right now, I would be looking at a contract. I was on fire, I was the champion, I was...

"Are you recording this?"

"What the hell do you think? This is some funny shit, it's going on YouTube!"

We stilled, my hands pulling chunks from Archie's head and his fingers wedged up my nose. "God, is that you?" Archie called out fearfully.

"I'm dying here," came a familiar voice, one that was being drowned out by the sounds of howling laughter.

Archie moved enough for me to look around him and then I groaned. Ben was leaning against a lamppost, shaking his head and chuckling quietly. Next to him, was the bent over form of Daniel, phone in hand pointed straight at us and tears running down his face.

"Make it stop, I can't breathe," he laughed, nearly falling over as he tried to get back upright.

"Who the fuck is this clown and why is he laughing?" Archie snarled, trying to get himself out of the bush and failing miserably as he collapsed back on top of me.

"Shut up, it's Willow's best friend."

Archie wiggled his way backwards, tumbling to the pavement flat on his back. He stayed there, groaning, not even thinking about me.

"Here."

A hand shot out in front of my face and I latched on. I literally flew through the air as Ben hauled me out of my ferny prison. I would have to ask him where he worked out later.

"I play rugby with Jason."

Fuck, did I say that out loud?

"Yes, you did," he chuckled.

This is some fucked up Jedi mind trick bullshit.

"I wouldn't go that far. That would be awesome though," he continued thoughtfully.

I wonder if...

"Ok, I'm bored now. Assume everything you think you're saying in your head is actually coming out of your mouth, ok sugartits?"

I glared at Daniel and thought about putting that theory to the test, but he rolled his eyes and turned to walk back to a car that was idling at the curb.

"Enough of this bollocks. Both of you get in the car, and I swear if you hurl on my leather seats, I'll kick both of your fucking arses."

Ben helped a limping Archie to get in as he grumbled, "You and who's fucking army?"

Ben and Daniel shared a look, and I didn't like the smirk they shared. "We don't need an army. We have an Annie."

31 – Well, that told me!

Willow

My eyes opened, and I immediately felt comforted. My old room looked the same as the day I moved out. Grandma always maintained that Simone and I would have a home here, no matter what happened in our lives or how far away we were. I hadn't needed to stay here in years but yesterday had been so epically shit, I just wanted to escape it all for a while.

Grandma had opened the door, surprised at first but happy to see me. Then she wrapped me up in one of her famous hugs and that was it, I was lost. The tears had cascaded down my face in a torrent that I had no way of stopping and the whole embarrassing story came rushing out in a blur.

Bless her, my grandma just held me, let me cry it all out and then finally when I grew silent, she sat me down with a huge mug of tea and the best cheese and ham toastie a girl could ask for. She didn't offer any advice, didn't even comment on the saga. She just snuggled up with me on her sofa and we watched tv until it was time to go to bed. I had missed being with her. It made me realise that I didn't spend enough time visiting. She deserved better than that after she had taken me in and been more of a parent to me than my own.

I swung myself out of bed and after using the bathroom, I made my way downstairs to the smell of freshly brewed tea and toast.

"Good morning poppet." She brushed a kiss across my temple and ushered me into a seat at the breakfast table. Grandma's house wasn't big by any means, but it was cosy, and clean and always welcoming. She always insisted on having breakfast together when Simone and I had lived here, saying it was the right way to set yourself up for the day, sharing a meal with those that mattered the most for you never knew what the day was going to bring.

I tried not to dwell on the fact that I ate breakfast alone most mornings. That was my own doing. I could be living here, I could be living with Simone and Daniel like they were always trying to get me to do, but I had wanted my independence. I hadn't realised until this moment just how isolated that had made me.

I had just popped the last bite into my mouth when grandma cleared her throat. "Ok, I think it's time we got down to business."

I swallowed thickly and gave a small nod. I gave her a lot to think about last night and that hadn't been fair. I couldn't bear the thought of her hating Perry, so I was gearing up to defend him when she knocked the argument right out of me.

"Why in god's name doesn't anyone at work know about you having Tourette's?"

"Grandma…"

She held a hand up to silence me. "You got to say your piece last night, now I think it's time you listened."

I sat still, my mug halfway to my lips and gave a resigned nod.

"You always assume people are going to think the worst of you, I blame your good for nothing parents for that. I thought you understood that they aren't the benchmark for normal in this

204

world, more like the benchmark for stupid."

She smiled knowingly. It was no secret that she didn't have any time for her daughter and her husband, not after the way they had made me feel. She barely spoke to either of them as far as I was aware, only when it was necessary. It was something that I had always been insanely grateful for, that she had taken my side for all these years but at the same time, I couldn't help the guilty feeling that if it wasn't for me, it would be a different story.

"And you can take that look off your face right now young lady. Those two are made for each other, I doubt things would be any different if you hadn't had obstacles to overcome."

"I didn't say a word," I spluttered.

"You didn't have to," she chuckled.

I took a sip of tea and mulled it over. She was most likely right, she usually was. It was just hard to accept.

"Now, back to you. I understand that you don't like it when people know all about your business, but it seems to me like you've put yourself under unnecessary pressure. God, I hate to think what you go through, having to suppress yourself all day. That isn't a way to live Willow. If the people you work with knew more, they would be understanding. It's not like you're contagious!"

She laughed, and I couldn't help but join her. "You really think that?"

She sobered and reached across to hold my hand. "I think you need to give more credit to human kind. There will always be exceptions. There will always be stupidity, uninformed minds and just plain arseholes. Luckily, they take up a small percentage of this world. Can you honestly sit there and tell me one person at work that you think would give you a tough time?"

I couldn't. I got on well with everyone in my department. Or at least I had until that evil woman had made an appearance yesterday. Now I didn't have a clue what to expect from them. Who knows what they were all thinking about me?

"My advice, for what it's worth, talk to them. People tend to be more inquisitive than anything else. You have nothing to lose and everything to gain. Imagine how much easier it would be to just be yourself and not come home feeling tighter than a spring every day."

Could I do this? I hadn't been open with people for a long time, just choosing to flash my phone at strangers in the street. But this was different, grandma was right. And if things got too hard, at least I would know I had done everything I could.

"Besides, isn't there like a code of conduct that everyone has to abide by?"

I rolled my eyes and smiled. "Yes, there is. When did you get so wise?"

"About the time I had to deal with two wayward teenage girls that wanted to turn my hair grey before my time."

I chuckled, drained the last of my drink and stood from the table. "Thanks grandma, I'd better get going or I'll be late for work."

"Oh no you don't young lady, that's taken care of. We aren't done here."

"What do you mean taken care of."

She busied herself tidying up the breakfast things. "I had a lovely talk with that delightful Ben and his wife Jasmine this morning. They know you're going to be a little late this morning. So, sit down," she ordered as I opened my mouth, mortified, to complain.

"Now, this Perry fellow. He treats you right?"

"Yes of course."

"He knows about you?"

"Yes but..."

"And you like him?"

I dropped my head to hide the smile that crept onto my face whenever he was mentioned. "Yes."

"Then why in god's name do you have more than 60 missed calls and over 100 unread text messages from the poor boy on your phone?"

I gasped. "You looked at my phone?"

She waved her hand dismissively. "Of course. Now, let's get something straight shall we? It's hard enough to find the right man, why would you push away the one that's perfect for you?"

"I never said he was perfect for me." My arms crossed defensively.

She mimicked my pose. "Any man that sings 'Unchained melody' down the phone, sends you pictures of himself pining outside your house and leaves voice clips on messenger telling you how much he misses you, wants to see you, will do anything to make this all right... I would say he's a little crazy for you. Or just plain crazy. But he's a handsome man, looks well built if you know what I mean so that overrides a little insanity."

"Grandma!"

I jumped to my feet and scurried into the

front room to retrieve my phone from my bag. Grandma may have exaggerated the numbers but sure enough, it had been blown up with messages and calls, mostly from him but from Simone, Daniel, Annie, Owen and Jasmine too. I felt a little choked up as I sat there, trawling through them all. I picked the last voice clip from Perry and hit play.

"I know being with me isn't easy, and it fucking should be. My parents, my crazy stalker... they aren't us Willow. I don't know how I can prove to you that what anyone says, or thinks doesn't matter to me. Only you baby, only you. I don't know what I have to do to make this right, but I'll find a way, I won't stop until I make you realise that you and me? We're the real deal. I never thought I'd feel this way about anyone and now that I have you, I'm never going to let you go. I'll fight for us Willow because I l..."

The message stopped abruptly. I sat there in shocked silence. Was he about to say...?

"Well?"

I jumped and turned to face my grandmother, a goofy smile on my face. "I think I need to get ready for work."

Her face lit up. "There's my girl. Go get your man."

32 – At least she's on my side

Perry

Someone had parked a lorry on my head. That was the only explanation I had for why I couldn't lift it. There was a droning noise close by, getting louder by the second. No, wait, it was more like a snuffling...

"What the fuck?"

Something wet was poking in my ear. My arms flailed about until one of them connected with something furry... and growling. I shot up, my head throbbing, my tongue thick and heavy and what the hell was that taste in my mouth?

"Daddy! He's awake! Can I watch cartoons now?"

One eye peeled itself open. I was on the floor in someone's living room with a blanket thrown over me and a lump lying next to me. The lump groaned and rolled over before resuming the droning sound. How the hell could Archie sleep through this?

An adorable little face with chubby cheeks, hazelnut eyes and ringlets watched me intensely. So did the huge mound of fur sitting at her feet with its teeth bared in my direction.

"I heard Daddy say you were shitfaced. My name's Kady and this is Snowy."

Snowy, the cutely named Husky, growled again for good measure before nudging his disgusting wet nose at the gorgeous little girl. She rolled her eyes, reminding me of Willow and gave him a stroke.

"I'm Perry."

"No you're not, my Daddy said you were

shitfaced."

"Kady! What have I told you about not repeating what Daddy says?"

Simone came charging into the room, her long black hair swept up into a bun and looking fresh faced and ready to face the day. The little girl sighed and looked up at her. "Daddy says naughty words, that's why he doesn't get presents from Santa. I won't get them either if I say them. But Mummy," she implored. "Daddy said that was his name!"

Daniel strolled into the room with two mugs in his hands and dropped a kiss to his scowling wife as he passed. "You're right baby, I did. But I was being silly. This is Perry."

Her mouth formed a little 'o' and then she jumped up and ran to the fireplace. "Sorry Santa, it won't happen again!" she yelled.

Kady hot footed it out of the room, thankfully taking the demon dog with her. Daniel passed a mug to me and chuckled. "Until next time. I swear that girl knows exactly what she's doing."

"Yeah, can't think where she gets that from huh?" Simone grabbed up a rucksack and left the room, but not before casting a curious glance in my direction. I could see she was going to say something and I was a little surprised she didn't lay into me.

"Thanks," I mumbled, lifting the mug to my lips. "On a scale of one to ten, how much does she want to kill me right now?"

Daniel frowned. "Simone? She doesn't. Why would she want to do that?"

Chuckling, or maybe it was a groan, I dragged myself off the floor and plopped down onto the sofa. "Because I've made Willow's life miserable."

He blew out a noisy breath and sat in the armchair. "How exactly do you think you've done that?"

"Is that a joke?"

"Nope," he declared, popping the p. "As far as I can see, Willow has been the happiest I've ever known her since you fell into her life. Ok, maybe not to begin with, but since you two have been bumping uglies..."

"Hey!" I growled, doing a much better job than Snowy.

He held a hand up in peace. "I'm just saying, you obviously care about her. Why would we have an issue with that?"

"Are you fucking kidding me!"

"Mummy, Shitfaced swore!"

Daniel winced. "Ok, now she might have an issue with you."

Looking around, I couldn't even see where the little voice had come from. It was creepy. Making a mental note not to curse, I attempted to point out all the many reasons why Willow was having a tough time, thanks to me but Simone walked in and placed herself on Daniel's lap.

"Yesterday, was not your fault. That woman, was not your fault. Willow's tic attack, again, not your fault."

"But..."

"No but's. Willow has a condition that sometimes wins the battle, it really is as simple as that. Yesterday was a lot for her to handle and she retreated to lick her wounds. She needed to do that for her, but that again, is not your fault. Now I love my cousin, we're as close

211

as sisters but I don't agree with the way she tries to deal with everything on her own. Luckily, she went to the right person for once and I know she's getting a good talking to as we speak."

That didn't sound good, especially when I saw the gleam in Daniel's eye. "Do I even want to know?"

"Relax," she laughed. "It's not like she's meeting with the devil. She went to Grandma's."

Sounded innocent enough but why did I suspect she wasn't a frail little old lady?

"As for you, get your shit together."

"Excuse me?"

Simone stood and towered above me. "Go home and get showered because you smell like a brewery. Take that brother of yours too and tell him to talk to my face next time we meet, not my boobs or I'll knock him the fuck out. Go and make sure Willow isn't walking into a whispering office this morning and for god's sake, ring your bloody mother!"

I couldn't remember ever feeling so small. It was like school all over again. "What about Amelia?"

Simone cackled, and I swear the sound was that frightening, my balls shrivelled up and took shelter.

"Oh, believe me, that bitch is taken care of."

She left the room. I gulped and looked at Daniel who was leaning back in his chair, watching his wife's arse as she sauntered down the hallway. "Fucking hell, she's incredible."

My eyes widened as he gripped his crotch and groaned.

Yeah, I wasn't having this conversation. I was

just thankful Willow was a little on the mellower side than her cousin.

"What does she mean, taken care of?"

He laughed maniacally. "You'll see my friend... you'll see."

✓✓✓

I was not popular right now, that much was blatantly obvious. Not one person had said good morning to me, instead they had all glared like I was the devil himself. Even the office smart arse, you know the one, had given me a frosty eyed glare. Not a high-five in sight. And the office gossips? Those girls wouldn't even look at me, instead turning in their chairs and crossing their arms defiantly.

And I couldn't be fucking happier about it. Because if they were angry with me, it meant they sided with Willow.

I waited for all the staff to be in, wishing Willow was going to be here too but from the email Jasmine had sent me, that wasn't going to happen. Instead I was going to have to face my department on my own.

Super.

Silence fell over the room as I stepped out of my office. I wasn't quite sure what the protocol for something like this was but for now, I was just going to have to wing it.

"Can you all pull up a chair please, we need to have an office meeting."

No one moved. I had half expected that to be the case, however, I was still their manager and I wasn't about to let them walk all over me. I

213

stared down whoever I could and one by one they all filtered over. Begrudgingly, but still they came. The quiet was deafening.

"Yesterday was..." I blew out a breath and glanced around. They didn't want to listen to corporate bullshit right now and quite frankly, I wasn't in the mood to give it. "It was shit, ok. That *woman,* the one that claimed to be my fiancé is a selfish, spoilt, manipulative bitch. I want you all to know that even if there was no one else in my life, I wouldn't touch her with a barge pole."

"Yeah, I'll bet your *barge pole* never went there."

And there was the office smartarse. "Rob, I wouldn't touch her with *your* barge pole, let alone mine."

There was some snickering and a few smirks dotted around, mostly from the guys. The women however, looked ready to lynch me. Not quite the direction I had been going for. "Look, I don't want to have a tell all about my love life, I think you've all heard enough for one year. I just needed to make it clear that she is a nasty woman and the only reason she came here yesterday was to cause problems for me and Willow."

"She said some awful things about Willow."

I turned to face one of the gossips, a forty something lady called Judy who was harmless. She looked upset. "It was a horrible thing to do Mr Moore."

"I know, I just wish I had been there when it happened."

Olive in the back piped up. "Mrs Hope cut her down to size, I was there. That woman got

214

thrown out on her arse. I've never seen Mrs Hope look so furious."

"I saw it too," another person said and before long, everyone was chucking in their comments on how Jasmine was epic and dealt with the dragon. It was crazy. I kept expecting Jeremy Kyle to jump in with his take on the subject. At least it would seem, they didn't all want to kill me anymore.

"But I don't get it. How could you be involved with someone so hideous? She was so vile; how could she just walk into our office and call someone out for being mentally handicapped like that?"

I opened my mouth to try to defend myself, but someone beat me to it.

"Because no matter how much he tries, Perry just can't seem to make the cow go away."

All eyes flashed to the door and my heart stopped beating. There stood Willow, looking as gorgeous as I had ever seen her in a short pinstriped skirt, her hair wild and curly just like I loved and... oh fuck me. Those red, shiny skyscraper shoes. Be still my beating cock.

"And just so you know... I prefer the term Tourette's Syndrome."

33 – We are family

Willow

"So, do you think I have it too?"

Laughing, I cocked my head to the side and studied Rob. "I would have to go with no."

"Are you sure? Because that would be awesome. I really think I could get away with saying I had that, what did you call it? Coprolalia?"

Owen rolled his eyes and slapped Rob on the back. "Just because you shout *get your fucking tits out* to any bit of jailbait that walks past, doesn't mean you have Tourette's."

"Yeah," Olive piped up as she walked by. "It just means you're a pervert."

Rob ran to catch up with her, trying to fight his corner and I stifled another laugh.

"That went well," Owen said.

It really did. I just spent the last 45 minutes giving my co-workers a run down on what my condition entailed, and they had been amazing. I had answered a ton of questions, some funny, some more serious but most importantly, all of them had been genuinely interested and accepting. I felt a huge weight lifted off my shoulders. I knew it didn't mean I would be entirely comfortable in the office, old habits die hard after all, but at least I wouldn't have the feeling of dread hanging over my head every time I felt the need to tic.

It also meant my toilet break escapes would be less frequent. One of the girls had even commented that she thought I had a bladder control problem, or maybe I went to secretly cry.

Made me realise things could been a whole lot worse. I could have been called Weeping Willow.

Owen pulled me in for a hug. "I'm so proud of you."

He released me before I could thank him and sauntered off to his desk. That just left me and Perry standing at the front of the office. I looked over my shoulder, already feeling the weight of his stare. There was a lot to say but I didn't really want it to be done here.

He held a hand out for me, but it represented so much more. I grasped it, not an ounce of hesitation and smiled broadly.

"Hey," he whispered.

"Hey," I whispered back.

He looked deeply into my eyes, and it felt like he was seeing right into the heart of me. It was a feeling that had scared me at first but now, I couldn't imagine not knowing what it felt like to have someone truly know who I was.

He leant closer, electricity pulsing between us. It was so strong, the urge to get as close as possible to him, to wrap myself in his arms and never leave...

"I fucking love those heels."

I threw my head back and laughed, deep, endless chuckles that spread through the room and had people smiling at us from every inch of the office. *Of course* he loved these shoes.

He attempted to pull me back towards his office, but I held my ground and shook my head. Worry flitted across his face, but I was quick to stop that in its tracks.

"No, we have the day off. I cleared it with Jasmine earlier."

He cocked his head to the side. "Ok, I'll bite.

What are we doing?"

"You'll see."

✔✔✔

"Left?"

"Yes, right up ahead."

"Why are we going left?"

"I told you. We're having lunch."

He frowned but made the turn while I just sat there getting more nervous by the minute. I couldn't believe he hadn't called me out on this yet. There wasn't much on this road, well, restaurant wise that is. But we weren't going to a restaurant, although I suspected the food would rival any Michelin star place.

"Take the second road on the right..."

"Willow," he growled. "What the hell have you done!"

I shrugged and placed a hand on his leg. "Something that you should have done weeks ago."

He sighed, propping his arm on the rest and rubbing at his temple. "I don't want to put you through this again."

Exasperated, I removed my hand and gave his arm a sharp thwack.

"What is with the beatings I keep getting from you women."

"Man up Reginald!" he narrowed his eyes at me but wisely didn't comment. "Now take the road on the left and follow it around the bend. First driveway on the left. You may have been there before, you know, every day until you moved out?"

218

He muttered under his breath but followed my directions. A few moments later we found ourselves trailing up the long gravel driveway and looking up at the gorgeous house he had grown up in. It was even grander to see in the daylight. Where before it had seemed like a fortress, now it looked more like a small castle. I guessed that was the look his parents had been going for.

We pulled up in front of the large porch and he kept the car running. For a split second he looked like he was going to make a break for it. Then, he turned the key and silence enveloped us.

"If this doesn't go well..."

"Then we just won't come back here. But Perry, at least we'll know that we tried."

He reached for my hand and raised it to my lips. "Does this mean there is still an us?"

My thumb grazed along the stubble on his cheek. "Would I be here if there wasn't?"

His eyes darkened, a look I knew all too well. Oh god, no way was I letting this happen in front of his parents' house!

"Bollocks," he groaned, looking over my shoulder. His dark, seductive expression changed dramatically into shock, then adorable confusion. "What the fuck?"

Panic flared as I turned in my seat, expecting to find Amelia standing arm and arm with his mother or worse, a restraining order to keep me away from them. *Nice going Willow, just freak yourself out right before you attempt a do over with the in laws from hell.*

Perry was already out of the car and opening my door for me, so I got out, took his hand and tried to see what had him so spooked. His mum and dad stood out on the porch, hand in hand and looking quite anxious. Well his mother did. His dad looked just as relaxed as the last time we had met.

We barely made it to the top of the steps when his mum broke away and lunged for me. I froze. Was she going to strangle me? Oh god, should I hit her back? What the hell was going on? What was the etiquette for punching out a middle-aged woman?

"My turkey won the basting contest!" *Kill me... kill me now!*

"I was so worried about you darling girl. Thank god you're alright." She crooned, completely ignoring my slip.

"Ummm," I couldn't even raise my arms to hug her back, she had such a tight grip on me. "I'm sorry?"

"Don't be sorry," his dad cut in, stepping up and wrapping his huge frame around the pair of us. "We're just so glad you're ok."

"You're wearing jeans!" Perry accused, staring pointedly at her legs.

"Yes, I'm well aware of that son. I dressed myself this morning you know."

"Ok, what in the actual fuck is going on here." Perry yelled.

"Reginald!" his mother scolded. "That language, honestly. Were you raised in the streets?"

And there she was. She let me go but didn't move far. Her arm wound around my waist as she guided me into the house. I could hear Perry quizzing his dad behind me, but they were talking too low for me to make out exactly what was being said.

"I've made your favourite for lunch Willow. Would you believe this was always Reginald's favourite when he was a child? He couldn't get enough of my Lasagne and homemade garlic bread."

"How did you know..."

"Oh, I asked Stephanie, I swear that girl knows everything."

"You talked to Annie?" Perry dodged around us and stood arms crossed in our path.

"Yes dear, I went to her house last night with your father," she leaned in close to me and whispered. "Her son is adorable."

I opened my mouth to answer but my pouting boyfriend wasn't done with his interrogation. "You better not have been rude to her, Mum. Annie is my best friend and if..."

"Oh, for goodness sake, I'm not a monster!"

His eyebrows rose in challenge. Out of nowhere, his dad slapped him around the head. "Watch that tone with your mother."

"I didn't say a bloody word!" he spluttered.

"Language!" his parents both shouted at the same time and I couldn't help it, I burst out laughing.

Perry's mum, who insisted I call her Belinda, ushered me through the house and into the huge kitchen that ran the entire width of the back. It was an incredible mix of farmhouse and modern-day fixtures, almost retro and so spacious. I ran my fingers along the countertop and dreamily thought of all the dishes I could bake with this kind of room.

"Do you like to cook?" Belinda asked as she fastened a pretty apron around her waist.

"I love to cook but I don't do it very often. I tend to end up making short, simple dishes."

"Why's that dear?"

Here we go, all or nothing. "Well, because sometimes my motor tics catch me off guard and I live alone so I have to be safety conscious."

She paused a fraction, a tray of fragrant dough on the tray in her hands. "Have you hurt yourself before?"

Nodding, I walked over and opened the oven door for her. "Yes unfortunately. I've slipped with a knife a few times but nothing more serious than a cut. I'm more likely to burn myself than anything else."

I held out my hands and showed her the movements my finger tics tend to make. "I've dropped a lot of things due to this, a couple of times it was a hot saucepan I was carrying."

I lifted my leg slightly and pointed to the faint burn scars that were obvious if you knew where to look. She gasped, and her hand flew to her mouth.

"Oh Willow."

"It's fine. I appreciate that I've been very lucky not to cause more damage to myself, so I don't push my luck."

She smiled and shook her head. "You're a remarkable woman Willow."

Perry and Alexander came into the room still talking quietly to themselves, but I could see that Perry was feeling a little more relaxed. Alexander started making drinks for everyone while making small talk and although it was a simple scene, I had a feeling there was going to be a lot more said as the day went on.

And I was right. We had barely cut into the lasagne, which was to die for by the way, when Belinda started the ball rolling.

"I had no idea Amelia had turned into such an awful person. I can't tell you how angry and disappointed I am with her."

"I tried to tell you," Perry mumbled.

"Yes well, you do have a knack for exaggerating."

He gasped, affronted and a little snicker left my lips. Seeing Perry pout like a teenager was fast becoming one of my favourite shows to watch. He narrowed his gaze at me and squeezed my thigh beneath the table.

"I had caught a little of the way she spoke to Willow that night. I had left the room to check on you dear, but got side tracked by the oven timer," she confided. "I was shocked and absolutely disgusted. I invited her here the next day to hear what she had to say for herself and she acted as if nothing had happened. She lied to my face."

Alexander was shaking his head solemnly. "Never thought for one minute she would be so cruel."

"Then I overheard her and Archie fighting and well, did you know she's been sleeping with your brother for years?"

Perry nearly choked on his garlic bread. "Um, yes. It may have come up."

She sighed sadly. "Any woman that would try to put brother against brother is a nasty piece of work. And all for the sake of her trust fund."

"It's fine, Mum. Honestly. He was welcome to her."

"Well, what goes around comes around."

Alexander laughed and placed a hand on his wife's shoulder. "You certainly made sure of that darling."

Our eyes darted back and forth between the pair of them as they laughed.

"What did you do?" I asked. I mean, who wouldn't?

"When Archie told us Amelia had behaved badly again at your work yesterday, I tried to get hold of Perry to find out what exactly had happened. When I couldn't reach him," she looked pointedly at her amused son. "I went to see Stephanie."

"It's Annie, mother."

"Yes, I know, and you're Perry. Why you kids shorten your birth names like that is totally beyond me."

"Mum!"

"That lovely Jasmine was at the house and told me all about what had happened, and I was so angry, I decided she needed to be dealt with. So, I went to see her father."

My eyes widened. "No way!"

She grinned and leant forward. "Oh yes."

"It's quite the scandal you know." Alexander reached for another slice of bread as if this was any ordinary conversation. "Amelia's father knows the affect that kind of behaviour could have on his reputation. He's taken her in hand."

"Oh, and just for good measure," Belinda whispered conspiratorially. "I said if that girl came anywhere near any of our family, or those that we love again, or indeed interfered in our lives in any way in the future, I would tell his wife that's he's been having sex with the 19-year-old twins that live across the road."

"Hang on, what twins?" Perry had his head cocked to the side. "The only twins I can think of are Stephen and Christopher."

Belinda's steady gaze held her son's and the penny dropped for us both at the same time. "Wow. That's uh... some secret weapon there Belinda."

"It really is." She held up her glass and toasted with Alexander. I couldn't help but feel grateful that for now I seemed to be on the right side of that woman.

34 – What doesn't kill us...

Perry

I hugged my mum on the porch and for the first time in I didn't know how long, I was sad to say goodbye. It had been an eye-opening day. She had been more welcoming and warm than I could remember in years. The effort she had made with Willow was more than I could have ever hoped for and more than that, she seemed to be genuinely interested in my girlfriend.

I never thought I would be someone that needed approval from his parents, and in truth, there wasn't a force on earth that would stop me from being with Willow. But to have their seal of approval just made it all that much sweeter.

"Now, if you want to have a potter about in the kitchen, you just come on over. I would love to have someone to share my love of cooking with."

"Are you gonna teach me how to make that garlic bread?" Willow asked slyly.

Mum threw her head back laughing. "We'll see."

Dad prised my girl from her arms and gave her one of his bear hugs. Mum had her hands in her back pockets and I just couldn't take it any longer.

"I haven't seen you looking so casual in years, Mum. What gives?"

She blew out a little huff and shrugged her shoulders. "We're not getting any younger Perry. It's about time we relaxed a little and enjoyed life. Your dad has dropped down to four days a week at work and I've handed the reigns over to half the clubs and charities I ran. We feel like brand new people."

"Aww you called me Perry."

"Yes I did, but don't get used to it."

We shared a smile. "They look good on you Mum."

I opened the car door for Willow and waved before we made the trek down the driveway. I couldn't believe it had gone so well today and it was all down to the amazing woman sitting next to me. If she hadn't forced me to go there and talk to them, I hate to think what would have happened to our relationship.

Willow was quiet, in fact she didn't say a word the entire drive back to her flat. Then again, neither did I. I was lost in my thoughts to the point that it didn't really register when we'd arrived at her flat, at least it didn't until I heard the car door shutting and saw her walking up her path.

I scrambled after her, catching up as she put her code in and pushed the door open. I caught it and followed her in like a lost puppy, which wasn't far from the truth. She didn't tell me to leave and that was good enough for me. When we reached her door she simply unlocked it and went through, not holding it for me but not slamming it in my face either.

I wasn't sure what was going through her mind, but I would wait it out. She had earned the right to take her time. We were finally on our own and there was so much to say. I expected her to drop onto the sofa, but she didn't. She bypassed the kitchen and headed towards her bedroom, shucking her coat as she went. Now I was in a dilemma. I wanted to follow but was that what she needed?

I could hear her telling her door frame off and just that simple act had me smiling. She wasn't totally out of it after all.

"Fuck it," I grumbled, dropping my own coat over the chair and kicking off my shoes. I stalked down the hall like a man on a mission and stopped dead when I hit the arch to her room. She was standing in the middle, her tight as hell short skirt gone and just a set of silky green underwear covering her luscious curves.

And those goddamn shoes.

Her eyes met mine, deep amber pools of emotion that called out to me. "Willow, I..."

She shook her head and reached around to unclasp her bra. It slipped from her arms and hit the floor at her feet. My eyes darted up to her face, trying gallantly not to focus in on the dark dusky nipples that would have my cock jumping for joy.

She ran her hands down her sides, the tips of her fingers latching onto the band of her pretty knickers. She toyed with them for a few seconds and then slowly, painstakingly, she lowered them down her shapely legs. My eyes lost the challenge and followed their journey, watching as she stepped out of them and closed the distance between us.

"Yesterday was," she whispered, "one of the shittiest days of my life."

My heart sunk with each word. "Will..."

"I've never had anyone be so openly rude, so unimaginatively uninformed and crass before."

"Baby..."

"It was brutal, Perry."

My head lowered in shame.

"It made me realise something very important."

My eyes closed as I waited for her to tell me it was over. That any chance for us was out of reach and all the apologies in the world wouldn't erase the shit that bitch had thrown at her. Shit she had to put up with, because of me.

"What we have is even more incredible than I already thought."

Hope burst to life in my heart, just as a very sexy, very naked Willow threw herself at me and attached herself to my lips. My body caught up with the situation a lot faster than my mind did. My shirt was being wrenched from my trousers, the buttons popping open with haste as she deepened her kiss.

She drew back slightly so she could watch as the cotton fell to the floor behind me and then her hands reached out to my chest. She moved her hands over my skin, her nails digging in slightly to the flesh and I felt it all the way down to my very excited cock.

I tried to move back in for another kiss, but she had other ideas. Before my eyes she dropped to her knees and looked back up with a look across that sexy face that would have a monk begging for action. Slowly, her hands slid down my body until they reached the button on my slacks. A little smirk grazed her lips as she slipped the disc through the hole.

Breath catching in my throat, I brought my hand to her face and caressed the soft, caramel skin. All I had wanted was to feel her in my arms, but she wasn't going to be satisfied with that tonight. I knew it the minute she slid my steel like cock into the wet, warm cavern of her mouth and slowly started to massage the sensitive underside with her tongue. I didn't know who the fuck had taught this woman to give head, but he deserved a medal. And a punch to the face. Right now, I was leaning more towards the medal.

"Holy fucking shit," I yelled when she pushed my dick to the roof of her mouth and went to town on the sensitive underside. If she kept this up, I was going to blow. Sliding myself free, I ignored the pout she aimed my way and hauled her up into my arms.

"I was enjoying that."

Chuckling, I carried her to the bed and laid us both down, side by side. "I need to say a few things before we go any further."

She chewed on her lip and I was immediately jealous of her teeth. What the hell was up with that?

"I think you're a very brave woman, Willow. I don't know what I did to deserve you but thank fuck I did. I know it hasn't been easy, being with me. But if you'll give us the chance..."

She placed her fingers over my lips. "No, stop right there. You've done everything right. Perry, I was hiding, not living, and I didn't even realise it. I've had more emotional upheaval in the last 6 weeks than I've had in the last 6 years, and it's made me realise a few things. I deserve to be happy and you? You make me the happiest. So, if you still want to have my crazy arse in your life, I'm yours."

"Well...," I drawled, milking the moment. "I always wondered what it would be like to date a stripper!"

Laughing, she curled herself a little closer to me and reached a hand up to cup my cheek. "I come with a lot of instructions and it isn't something I can compromise with. I have good days and bad days. I will embarrass us both from time to time and there will always be the Amelia's of the world that refuse to understand. I will be mocked, sometimes you will too, just for being with me."

"I'll kick their arses..."

"No," she smiled a little. "You can't change the world Perry. Just remember that for every unkind comment, there are ten more kind ones."

Awed by her outlook, my eyes roamed her face in wonder. "I'll do my best. Not promising anything though."

She glanced down and took a steadying breath. "There is also the fact that, if we... if I have children, it's possible they will develop the syndrome too."

"I can't think of anything more adorable than a few mini Willows running around and shouting at the furniture."

"You say that now," she giggled.

"We'd have to buy some chickens."

"And a turkey!"

"You can have anything you want Willow, anything."

I couldn't hold back any longer. Pushing her back into the sheets, I covered her body with my own and lost myself in her. Every touch was like coming home, and I knew down in my soul that it was going to feel like that every time we touched for the rest of my life.

Look at me, a real-life Romeo!

Hours later we surfaced back to the real world, our bodies tangled in the sheets and exhausted smiles set in stone on our faces. She was drifting off to sleep. It was now or never.

"Kocham cie," I whispered into her ear.

She gasped, her body stilling. I waited patiently, hoping to god that Simone hadn't stitched me up and taught me the wrong phrase. The last thing I needed was the first time telling Willow *I love her*, actually be me telling her to fuck off in polish. That would suck balls.

She twisted around and propped her chin on my chest. "Did you really just say that?"

I squinted. "It depends on what I said."

"You said I look like a man."

"Fucking Simone, I'm gonna kill her..."

She giggled into my chest and shook her head. "I'm sorry, you didn't. You should have seen your face though."

I rolled us until I towered above her and scowled down at the hysterical woman that had turned a beautiful moment into a comedy act. "Woman! Is this what I have to expect every time I say I love you?"

She sobered and shook her head a little. "No, please say it again Perry."

I kept her waiting, but not for long. I wasn't stupid after all. "I love you, Willow."

"Perry," she breathed. *"Kocham cie.* I love you too, so much."

A tear slipped from the corner of her eye. "Well what are you waiting for? Kiss me Reginald!"

Epilogue

Willow

"I can't believe you made me come here."

Stifling my chuckles, I grabbed Perry's hand and dragged him through to the front of the packed club. Hot Steppers was hopping tonight, and we had our own table right there by the stage.

"You made it," Ben shouted over the ruckus.

He stood to kiss my cheek and shook hands with my boyfriend. Yup, I had a boyfriend now. I was still a little giddy every time I called him that. Although, the term was a little tame. He had practically moved in with me. He hadn't slept at Annie's in weeks and somehow all his washing had worked its way into my hamper. Not that I was complaining. I didn't want to be apart from him anymore than he did.

It had taken quite a bit of adjusting though. He had learnt to duck first thing in the morning when I made the tea, my finger flexes had a habit of flinging the cupboard door open. He learnt that the hard way. A bit like the lesson he got in grabbing the food from the fridge *before* I started my morning lecture on the appliances behaviour.

For me the strangest thing was having someone in my private space to witness all of this. He really was perfect though, I felt completely comfortable around him. Not once had he shown any sign of impatience, and that meant everything to me.

"Is he really going to go through with this?" Jasmine questioned. She laid a tray of drinks

233

on the table and took her seat on her husband's lap.

"Oh yeah, he has to," Annie shouted. "I didn't come all the way out here tonight for nothing. It was either this or I was going to shave his balls and send the video viral."

The lights dimmed, a red tint to the stage as the infamous mc spoke into the microphone.

"Ladies and gentleman, we have a new act for you tonight. He's big, he's strong... he's enough to turn you on!"

Hollers and whoops went up all around... a lot of them from our table.

"He's not gonna do it," Perry stated, crossing his arms over his chest. "I'm telling you now, I know my brother. He won't do this."

"He owes me big time," I reminded him and laughed when he once again scowled at the stage.

Archie had finally remembered where he knew me from. Of course, out of everywhere it could have been, it was my first show as *B'Twitched*. Perry had hoped his brother wouldn't make the connection. He also had to do some grovelling for not telling me Archie had been with him that night. I enjoyed that part.

Archie swore it was my smile that gave it away. I was happy to go along with that white lie, as was Perry. I think it was the only thing that saved Archie from getting his arse kicked by his brother.

He swore up and down that he would never tell a soul, but I had still been scared stiff that he would rat me out to Perry's folks. That was the last thing I wanted, especially now that we spent most Sunday's there. They had warmed so much and were so unbelievably supportive of our relationship, it would break my heart to lose it now.

So, to put my mind at ease, he had come up with this plan. I wasn't totally sure how this was going to make up for my embarrassing secret. He was a good-looking man, in good condition... I didn't know what was so bad about him stripping that it matched my own. Or at least I didn't.

"Please give it up for... So Macho!"

And there he was. A swaggering mass of curly haired wig, over the top moustache and garish shell suit took to the stage. He swayed his body flamboyantly to the beat, making a show of losing the shell suit and bam! Fluorescent leotard and matching legwarmers met the eye... and oh my god!

"That's got to be padding... right?" Jasmine whispered, albeit loudly.

As one, Simone, Jasmine, Annie and myself all tilted our heads to the side to study the enormous bulge in Archie's leotard.

"It's fake," Jason spluttered.

"It's a costume trick," Daniel deadpanned.

"I'm pretty sure I saw him stuffing sports socks down there," Ben declared.

All eyes turned to Perry who just leaned back in his chair confidently. "He takes after his brother."

✓✓✓

"I can't believe you did that," I laughed, clutching my sides and practically falling out of my seat.

Archie smiled, still sporting the wig and moustache but thankfully out of the legwarmers. They had been thrown into the crowd somewhere right before he whipped off the leotard and left a puddle of moist birds in the audience.

And yes, I actually shouted that.

One woman had screamed that she wanted the monster schlong to destroy her pussy... some things can't be unheard.

"Well, as long as we're even," Archie smiled, wriggling in his seat as another set of hands tried to get an 'accidental grope' as they wandered by.

"You know, it's just occurred to me that Annie and Jason are the only couple that hasn't taken a turn on the stage," Ben accused. "That doesn't seem fair."

Jason stood up and started to flex his muscles.

"I'd rather see him than Annie," Perry laughed. "That's just wrong."

Archie held his hand out for a fist bump, only to have Perry, Ben and Daniel join him.

Annie stood, affronted. "Hey! I'm a fucking vixen. My milkshake brings all the boys to the yard."

She started for the stage only to have her husband yank her back into his arms. "Not a chance little mama. You've already gone into labour once in this place, let's not make a habit of it."

The night had been fantastic, and I was feeling far happier now that Archie had made a fool of himself too. As we were leaving, I felt the usual tell-tale sign that I was about to do something I couldn't help and where I would usually fight to suppress it, I just let it happen.

My hand shot out and flicked the bouncer... right in his crotch. Well, that wasn't exactly what I thought was going to happen. He glanced down at me with a look crossed somewhere between amusement and shock but before I could flash my trusty phone screen at him, Perry beat me to it.

Phone shoved in his face, the bouncer stared at Perry's screen intently for precious seconds before turning his smiling face at me. He grinned wider and shook Perry's hand. "You're a lucky man."

Not saying a word, I was ushered out of the building where I spun around and demanded to see his phone. He handed it over immediately and watched my face as I read it.

***My girl has an ass that is fine
Her Tourette's kicks in some of the time
She'll kick you and flick you it's true
Shout poultry and polish at you
But keep your hands off, coz she's mine***

Hot tears built behind my eyes as the phone was passed around. He did that for me? I knew he wasn't embarrassed or ashamed of my condition, but this was something else.

We all said our goodbyes but all I could focus on was the man in front of me. Launching myself at him, I hugged him hard and sighed contentedly into his neck.

"How did I get so lucky?"

He chuckled. "I think it was me that got

237

lucky Willow."

He dropped his mouth to mine and I was lost. He was perfect for me and I was going to show him just how amazing I thought he was the minute we got home.

"I think I need a cock in my hen house."

He threw his head back and laughed. "Yeah let's go home... so I can nibble your giblets."

The End

Dork To Dirty

Want to see where it all began? Find out what happened when Jasmine met Ben... and a stripper called Dork To Dirty!

"Those of you in the Hot Steppers club will be glad you were here this evening I promise you that. They call him – the tech with the torso...."
A woman screamed in the back.
".... They say he knows a million ways to pleasure you...."
Whoops and hollers started from a massive crowd of ladies in the front.
".... oh you know where I'm going with this don't you ladies?"
Yeses and shouts of joy were echoing around the club as ladies everywhere started chanting.
"That's right ladies, hold onto your bras. For one night only and back by popular demand, we bring you.... From Dork to Dirty!"

Available at **Amazon**

Acknowledgements

Where to start!

I feel like Ticked has been in my head forever. I had lost count of how many times I'd started it... only to be distracted by life, Spiralling Ink, demanding children... but she's finally here!

Willow's story was something I was desperate to write, but a little frightened of too. Hours of research went in to making sure I did justice to those who live with Tourette's Syndrome. From the countless blogs I read and watched, to the insightful websites and meetings out there, one thing stuck with me – Tourette's is possibly one of the most misunderstood conditions. If you're interested in learning more, check out Tourette's hero dot com... it worked for Perry!

Ticked wouldn't be finished even now if it wasn't for an extremely pushy, motivational and supportive Smutter. Brittany, you kick my arse when it needs it, you pick me up when I'm down and when all else fails... you send me dodgy Snapchap videos! Thank you for always having my back, you crazy fool!

I couldn't do any of this without my Alpha Beta Julie. She's always meticulous with her notes, picks up all my plot holes and lack of capital letters (stupid computer hates me) but it's the style in which she does it that really has me dying. *"Uhhhh Karen? Pretty sure you've described a stalker!"* Thanks for keeping me on the straight and narrow Jules.

The amazing Lisa Reads at The Book Teaser Pleaser has done it again with the Ticked cover. As always, I'm in awe of her incredible talents.

She nailed Willow and Perry for me, and as for those teasers... don't get me started on the lack of interracial couples the stock photo world has to offer! But we got there in the end and they're hot as hell! Thanks my love, I'd be lost without you.

To the real life Gosia, my polish friend who patiently wrote out a ton of phrases for me – I will never be able to pronounce any of it without sounding like an idiot, but thank you so much for helping me.

Huge shout out to all the Sinful Smutters! You guys have me and my partners in crime, Brittany and Emily in stitches. May the group continue to grow.

And finally, to each and every one of you that picked Ticked up and gave it a chance, *Thank you!* Whether you loved it or hated it, I just want to say I appreciate you taking time out of your busy lives to dive into my book, it means the world to me.

Is this the end of the Don't Judge A Book Novels? Not a chance! There are many more faces destined to grace the stage at Hot Steppers... Just you wait.

Love you guys, catch you later

Karen xxx

About the Author

A self-confessed reading addict, Karen is usually found either writing or with her nose stuck in a book. Or Adulting because apparently, she should do that too sometimes! She's a lover of wildly inappropriate humour, has an addiction to swear words and bananas, lands her foot in her mouth daily... but she wouldn't have it any other way.
Karen can be summed up with 5 words: Friendly, loyal, thankful, funny and above all... Smutty!

Karen would love to hear from you and welcomes your feedback!
Please feel free to contact her at
authorkarenraines@gmail.com
www.karenraineswrites.com

It's even easier to connect with social media, come and find Karen at:
www.facebook.com/authorkarenraines
FB fan group Sinful Smutters
Twitter - @Karen_Raines_SI
Instagram - KARENRAINES_AUTHOR

Are you on Goodreads? Come and say Hi!

Reading List

Spiralling Ink Series
Loved: Kit's Spiral
Strength: Claire's Spiral
Control: Hayley's Spiral
Honest: Neil's Spiral (Coming Soon)

Don't Judge a Book Series
Dork to Dirty
A Dork Wedding
Ticked

Made in the USA
Columbia, SC
19 January 2018